I0757989

Books by Sara R. Cleveland

Penelope's Dragon
Saving the Dragon
Courting the Dragon

Bared Magic

Sara R. Cleveland

Content Warnings: Includes course language, physical violence, allusions to slavery, sexual abuse and assault.

For my husband.
I always sleep better by your side.

BARED MAGIC

In which Goldilocks discovers a
bed that is just right

The cottage was tucked so far back in the woods that she almost missed it. A cheeky ray of sun dared to pierce the thick canopy, bathing the structure's thatched roof in a wash of inviting, golden light. In that moment, it seemed a sign from the heavens. Wynne veered off the trail, her feet pounding a mad rhythm as she plunged through the underbrush. Her hand was just brushing the door's handle when the sound of her pursuers came crashing down the narrow forest path. She muttered a prayer and pushed on the door.

To Wynne's immense surprise, the door swung inward with ease. She darted inside and drove the bolt home before pressing her back to the door, listening. At first, it was hard to hear anything over the pounding of her own heart and ragged breaths. She forced herself to take long, slow pulls of air until some of the tension seeped out of her.

"Think the witch went inside?"

All the tension snapped back into her muscles, and Wynne stiffened against the thin oak planks. She wondered how much protection the door with its iron hinges but flimsy latch could truly offer. She held her breath as the door suddenly pressed into her back before rattling back on its hinges.

"Door's locked," the same voice said, much quieter this time. Wynne could picture the thug's cruel leer with its yellowed, crooked teeth. Some were missing, if she remembered correctly. Reminders of more than a few barroom brawls. She could almost imagine his ale-soaked breath on her neck as he added, "And I don't see no keyhole."

Wynne's eyes darted around the room, taking it in for the first time. A spare amount of sunlight filtered in through the gaps in the shutters, which—she noted with some relief—were latched from the inside. In front of her and to the right was a round dining table with three stout chairs. In the gloom beyond that, she could make out an iron stove and shelving that spoke of cooking and herb work.

The wall to the left featured a quaint hearth of river stone with a roughly hewn mantle. Three stools with tripod legs were scattered about a thick rug before the fireplace. What looked like fishing gear was piled in one corner while a curio cabinet filled the other.

Directly opposite where Wynne stood was a doorway. A woven tapestry featuring a hunting scene hung from the top of the door frame, blocking the room beyond from view.

"Go check around back," the thug's muffled voice whispered to his companion.

"There might be a door."

Panic flooded Wynne's veins. She forced herself to move towards the tapestry that hid the back of the house. What if there was another door? What if there were open windows?

The room beyond was darker than the front, with shutters better fitted to the windows. As Wynne's eyes adjusted, three large shapes resolved into beds positioned against the far wall, which thankfully did not appear to have a door.

Wynne's ears tracked the sounds of the other man creeping around the back of the house. He was quieter than the thug who had tried to grab her at the tavern. His image wasn't as clear in her mind, but Wynne remembered a vague impression of a weasel. When the small noises of his exploration started back around to the front of the cottage, Wynne crept back to the door to listen.

"No door. Windows are shut tight, too." His voice was raspy, like he hadn't had a drink in a week. "Either she's in there, or the inhabitants are taking a nice nap."

"You go back there in case she tries to sneak out a window," her would-be captor ordered. "I'll break down the door and drag her out."

"Are you insane?" his companion hissed. "Do you know who this cottage belongs to? They find out we broke in, and you won't have to worry about what the chit stole because you'll be worm food in a shallow grave."

If her heart wasn't already in her throat,

Wynne would have choked on it. Who was the owner of this cottage that they could terrify murderous malefactors like these? Was she jumping out of the frying pan and into the fire?

A guttural curse was followed by fading footsteps.

Wynne didn't believe for a second that they were giving up. She crept to a window. The crack between the shutters and the sill was just big enough to peer out. Both men were visible, standing several yards away and conversing quietly. Periodically, one of them would glance at the cottage. Finally, they separated, each finding a tree and sitting down with his back to it, eyes glued to the cottage.

"Damn." The curse escaped with her exhale, and Wynne jerked away from the window. Clearly, they were willing to wait for her or the return of the cottage's mysterious owners—whichever came strolling into the clearing first.

Wynne crept to the kitchen and examined the contents of the shelves. Perhaps she could learn something about her unwitting benefactors. Maybe she'd get lucky, and the owners of the cottage would forgive her trespassing under the circumstances. It could be that they even had a soft spot for desperate young women. After all, tucked away in the woods like this, the cottage could very well belong to a couple of capable hedge witches. Real hedge witches, the kind with the power to turn those sick bastards outside into frogs.

Nothing on the shelf indicated that anyone more interesting than a talented apothecary was in residence. Ordinary kitchen staples took up most of the space. A bag of flour branded with the mark of the local mill slumped against the wall. Another bag with the same branding proved to be filled with turnips.

As her terror gave way to curiosity, Wynne noticed a familiar aroma wafting through the cottage. Her nose led her to a pot resting on the iron stove. A thick leather mitt lined with quilted fabric sat on the shelf closest to the stove. Wynne slipped it on and lifted the heavy lid from the pot. An initial gust of steam made her recoil before leaning in and breathing deep—venison stew.

Her stomach grumbled.

"In for a penny, in for a pound," she muttered, setting the lid aside. She whipped off the mitt and turned back to the shelves to see what crockery was available. Three sets of earthenware dishes, each glazed in a different color, sat in a neat row. Each set had a large plate, a bowl, and a mug stacked in that order. A set of cutlery poked out of each mug. Wynne took the spoon and bowl from the stack with a rich, forest-green glaze.

She took her pilfered meal to the bedroom. Somehow, she didn't think she'd want to be sitting at the table, bold as you please, eating her unsuspecting hosts' dinner when they walked in. At least back here she'd have a chance to hide the evidence until they agreed to hear her out.

If they agreed to hear her out.

Wynne used one hand to guide her way along the bedroom wall while the other, swaddled in the oven mitt, cradled the piping hot bowl. She felt her way to the furthest bed to the left. It was hard to tell with almost no light, but Wynne thought the bed was a bit wider and longer than a single cot. It was certainly taller. Her hand sunk into the mattress. Featherbed. What an odd luxury to find in a cottage in the middle of the woods.

As soon as she sat down, a strange weariness sank into her like a weight, pinning her in place. Her eyes dropped immediately to half-mast. The bowl in her hands seemed unbearably heavy.

"Maybe I should just..." The thought was cut off by a yawn, and Wynne found herself falling sideways. Her head hit the goose-down pillow at the same time the bowl hit the floor. She should clean that up. She should...

"I can't wait to crawl into bed and sleep."

Callum snorted. Brodie would do nothing but sleep if their eldest brother, Alasdair, didn't threaten to beat the lazy out of him on a near-daily basis. Once, when they were all barely more than cubs, Alasdair had dumped a bucket of ice water on a sleeping Brodie around midwinter. The two of them had almost wrecked Momma's favorite chair in the ensuing fight.

"You can sleep when the working's done." Alasdair strolled into the clearing as if summoned by the very mention of Brodie sleeping. Moisture darkened his tawny hair, and his clothes clung to him like he'd put them on while his body was still damp. Two nice stringers of trout dangled from his meaty fist.

"We're working while you're off playing," Brodie grumbled, plunking another log of deadwood onto the stack he would tie up to carry back.

Alasdair raised one bushy golden eyebrow.

"We're just about done here, Al, don't worry," Callum put in before Alasdair could start on a lecture about the difference between fishing for food and a leisurely swim. He cinched the knot he was tying for emphasis. He had a nice, healthy bundle of deadwood to take back to the cottage. And if it was a little bigger than Brodie's? So be it.

The three of them made their way home in companionable silence that was occasionally punctuated by Brodie attempting to goad Alasdair into another sparring match. For a man who was supposedly so exhausted all the time, Brodie was awfully keen on a good brawl.

Callum paid them no mind. It seemed Brodie had been born for the special purpose of annoying Alasdair, and Callum had been born to ignore them.

Oh, but what he wouldn't give to be able to sleep like Brodie. Callum let himself daydream a bit. Early this morning, before even Alasdair had jumped out of bed, Callum had snuck out of the cottage. An old hedge witch lived a few miles away—nothing Callum couldn't run in an hour—who specialized in charms. Mostly love charms if the villagers' rumors were true. Callum didn't need a love charm, but he did need something that would let him get just one blessed full-night's rest. The little sachet had cost him a pretty penny, but the old witch had promised it would get him the rest he sought if he but placed it under his pillow before bed. She had strongly advised him against looking inside it, however.

He'd stuffed it in the designated hiding place before either of his brothers could see it, his nose twitching from the stink of the witch's magic. Callum hoped that neither of them would notice the scent and remark upon it. At least not until he'd gotten that night's rest he'd paid so dearly for. If this insomnia went on much longer, he just might finally go insane.

Callum nearly collided with Alasdair's back before he realized his brothers had stopped walking. Both of them were motionless, taut as bowstrings. Callum tensed and sniffed the air cautiously. The heavy scent of male sweat and chewing tobacco hung in the air. There was something else—something more delicate—underneath the acrid aroma, but Callum couldn't quite tell what it was.

"It seems we have company," Alasdair growled. He handed the trout to Callum. "I'll circle around to the west. Brodie, you go east. Callum, you know what to do."

Man melted into beast, and where the eldest brother had stood, a brown bear sat on its haunches.

"Excellent," Brodie said, dropping his bundle of firewood. "I love company."

Even in bear form, Alasdair managed to roll his eyes. Then two bears lumbered off into the forest, leaving Callum alone on the path with the firewood and the fish. He sighed and picked up Brodie's bundle. It wasn't far from the cottage, and stars knew when Brodie would come back for it.

Callum trudged the rest of the way to the cottage by himself, still very much a tall human man. This was their usual tactic. One brother would approach the trespassers as a man to determine their purpose. If necessary, back-up would come crashing in with claws swinging. Callum didn't mind being the bait, but he was starting to think his brothers thought he was a pack mule instead of a werebear.

Two men scrambled to their feet when Callum trudged into the clearing surrounding the cottage. They seemed vaguely familiar, but he didn't think they'd be introduced. These were just people he passed on the street when errands forced him into town. Callum walked right past them. Exposing his back was a calculated risk. He dropped the firewood by the front door and hung the fish from a peg in the wall.

"Can I help you, gentlemen?" he asked, turning back to his uninvited guests.

"We have reason to believe a thief has barricaded herself in your cottage," the taller man said. He was a big-boned man with bad teeth who liked to keep his scalp shaved to show off his tattoos. And probably to hide a receding hairline, Callum thought uncharitably.

"Is that so?" Callum made a show of folding his arms and studying the cottage for signs of anything amiss. "And what makes you think so?"

"We were tracking her. The trail led us here. The door's barred from the inside; she's barricaded herself in your home and probably robbed you blind in the process."

"Do you make a habit of trying other people's doors?"

"What?" The big man looked dumbfounded. Apparently, this wasn't the direction he'd expected the conversation to go.

The smaller man glanced nervously at Callum. Then his beady eyes darted away to scan the surrounding woods.

Callum took as deep a breath as he could without being obvious and almost gagged. Wereweasel. Well, that simplified things then.

"Go home, weasel. And take your friend with you. My brother's asleep in the house, and he won't be amused if we interrupt his nap."

The big man looked ready to argue, but the wereweasel put a restraining hand on his arm. "It's not worth it, Clint," he muttered, risking a glance at the werebear.

Callum graced them with a wide smile, showing off his unusually large canines.

"That's right, Clint. Go home. Or go chase after your mystery girl, I don't care. Just do it away from here. My brothers don't like trespassers. They won't be as friendly as I am."

The two shuffled from the clearing back towards the path. The wereweasel's eyes still scanned the trees, but the man named Clint kept throwing nasty glares over his shoulder at the cottage. When they were out of sight, a big brown bear ambled out of the woods.

Callum could tell from its size and the golden-brown of its fur that it was Alasdair. The bear stopped at his side, eyes trained on the path the strangers had taken. It stood up on its hind legs and in a blink, Alasdair stood in its place.

"Brodie is following them to make sure they head into town and don't circle back."

"Did you catch all of that?"

"Enough. So, we have a third visitor, eh?"

"So it would seem." Callum turned back to the cottage, studying the door. "I told you we should have gotten one of those fancy new locks."

"So one of you idiots can lose the key in the forest? No thanks."

The door was indeed bolted from the inside. Callum pushed against it half-heartedly before stepping back to eye the hinges critically. It wouldn't have taken much for those two to break down the door. It must have been the wereweasel's fear of reprisal that kept the louts out. He raised his fist.

"What are you doing?" Alasdair asked. Amusement colored the question.

"Hoping our guest will see sense and

unbolt the door. I'd rather not have to replace it if I don't have to."

Callum gave the door several sharp raps with his knuckles.

"Hello in there!" he called. "It seems you've mistaken our home for yours. Think you could let us in? I'd hate to break this door down."

Both brothers paused, ears pricked for even the slightest sound that would indicate movement. Nothing.

Callum knocked again, hard enough to make the door shake. "Hey, you really don't want us coming in there angry. Open up."

Alasdair laughed. "I don't think it's going to be that easy, Baby Bear. Step aside."

Callum rolled his eyes but got out of the way. He'd been body-slammed by Alasdair enough times to know he pitied the door. Alasdair backed away to get a running start, charging the door with his shoulder forward. The flimsy lock caved, and the door popped open beneath the big man's weight to hang crookedly inside the cottage from one valiant hinge.

Which was empty.

"Think they went out a back window?"

Alasdair shrugged. "Not many places to hide in here."

Callum breathed in the familiar scents of home. The venison stew they'd left simmering on the stove dominated the room, but he could pick up notes of drying herbs, fish guts on Alasdair's tackle in the corner, and the distinct musk of bear. Yet, there was something new in the bouquet. Something almost floral and very, very feminine.

"Well, there was definitely a woman here. I can smell her."

Alasdair took a deep whiff and nodded. He gestured towards the doorway opposite them. Bedroom?

They followed their noses. It was odd, but the smell of stew got stronger. Each stood on either side of the bedroom door. Alasdair pressed a finger to his lips, then held up three fingers. He slowly put one finger down at a time in a silent countdown. When he got to zero, he ripped the tapestry from its tacks. Sunlight from the open front door brought some illumination to the room.

The first thing Callum noticed was his bowl lying on the floor in a puddle of congealed stew. Its rim was chipped, and a new crack ran down its side. The second thing he noticed was a decidedly feminine hand dangling from the edge of his bed.

The light wasn't great, but Callum didn't need much to know she was beautiful. Hair like summer sunshine was spread out over his favorite pillow and freckles danced across the sun-kissed skin of her nose. Callum had the mad urge to kiss every one of them. He wondered what color her eyes were. Blue, perhaps? Whatever they were, it didn't matter. She was stunning. She was snoring.

She was snoring.

A low moan of regret escaped him before he could stop it. The woman had used up his sleeping charm. Three practically identical beds in the room, and the fool woman had chosen his.

Alasdair poked her cheek with one blunt finger. Her brow furrowed a bit, but she didn't otherwise stir.

"Amazing. She sleeps harder than Brodie."

Callum sighed and reached under the pillow. He opened his hand to reveal the sachet to his brother. "She doesn't have a choice. She's going to be zonked for at least eight hours. I bought this off Old Fiona this morning." He scratched his head sheepishly. "I knew you wouldn't approve, but... I just had to get some decent sleep."

2

In which the torches and pitchforks arrive

o you think she's ever going to wake up?"

Wynne's eyes shot open. She snapped into a seated position, and a cozy quilt dropped from her shoulders to her lap. She turned to find herself face to face with two pairs of warm brown eyes. Two men sat on another bed several feet away, staring at her with a mix of awe and amusement.

"Who are you? What am I doing here?" she asked.

"We were hoping you could tell us." One of the men leaned closer. A mop of burnished auburn hair shaded eyes the color of warm honey.

Wynne felt her face heat under the intensity of his gaze. She looked away, frantically searching her memory. Like stained glass breaking in reverse, the pieces of the afternoon flew back into place until a clear picture formed in her mind. The men. The chase. And then—

"I was being chased. I saw this house, and I ran inside, hoping they would run on by. They didn't." She pressed a hand to her forehead. "I remember putting stew in a bowl and coming back here to hide and then... nothing."

The man sighed, and Wynne looked up at him. Dark smudges, like bruises, weighed down his eyes. He looked like he hadn't slept in a week. Despite the exhaustion etched into his features, Wynne couldn't help but notice he was a handsome man. He had a rugged but boyish charm. A shadow of strawberry stubble added to his disheveled appeal.

"I'm afraid that last bit is my fault." He produced something from his shirt pocket. It was a small sachet of midnight blue silk. "This is—or was—a sleeping charm I bought from a hedge witch. It was supposed to make sure I got a good eight hours of rest tonight. Instead, you had a nice long nap." He sat up straight and tucked the defunct sleep charm back into his pocket. "You mind telling me why those men were chasing you?"

"It's complicated."

"So, make it uncomplicated," the other man said, folding his arms across his chest. He was leaner and darker than the tired man, his hair and eyes were a rich chocolate color—but the family resemblance was unmistakable. Brothers perhaps?

"The bald guy. I think he works at the tavern. He says I stole something from him."

The ginger leaned in again, his eyes locked with hers. "And did you?"

"No." Wynne kept her gaze steady and resisted the urge to fidget. She raised her chin, the set of her jaw defiant. "It didn't belong to him."

"I think you better show us what you took," the dark-haired one said. His easy expression had hardened into a frown.

"I can't."

"And why not?"

"Because I don't have it," she snapped. His scowl grew, and she softened her tone. She needed to convince these men that they should let her go. "I gave it back to its rightful owner."

"Well, that's awfully convenient."

"What's your name?" the first man asked, changing the subject before the conversation could spiral further down the wrong direction.

Wynne bit her lip. She'd known this question was coming. It was an obvious question, and someone with nothing to hide would answer it easily. Wynne might not be the thief that the bar thug claimed, but she had plenty to hide.

"Would you believe me if I said I don't want to tell you for your own good?"

This elicited an eye roll from the dark-haired man who stood so swiftly that Wynne cringed. "This is a waste of time. You have fun with Goldie here. I'm going to see if Alasdair needs help."

He strode from the room, somehow making dropping the tapestry back into place feel like a slamming door.

The other man shook his head. "Don't

mind Brodie. He doesn't have a patient bone in his body."

"So, there are three of you. Alasdair, Brodie, and..."

"Callum," he supplied. A faint smile turned up the corners of his mouth.

"You must be the youngest brother."

"What gave you that idea?"

"Alasdair, Brodie, Callum. A, B, C. Seems pretty on the nose, don't you think?"

Callum laughed, and Wynne had to reevaluate her original assessment. He wasn't just attractive when he really smiled; he was downright gorgeous.

"Momma had the next name all picked out. She wanted a girl, and she was going to call her Deirdre. And if she got a fourth hellion, then we would've had a Donald." He grinned. "Fortunately for all our sanity, I was the last."

"What time is it?" Wynne looked to the windows, but they were still shuttered tight. The two of them sat within the warm glow of an oil lamp.

"Late," he admitted. "Probably about midnight."

Wynne scrambled to her feet. "I'm so sorry. You probably want to go to sleep. I should go."

A warm hand caught her wrist. Wynne resisted the urge to pull away, but her heart leapt into her throat. She hadn't given him any of the answers he was looking for. What if they were planning to hold her overnight so they could take her back to the village in the morning?

"Wait," his voice was as gentle as his grip, which he released as soon as she stopped moving. "It's late, and the roads aren't safe. Especially since Clint and his weasel buddy may still be hanging around."

"Clint?"

"The bald man who was chasing you."

"Oh. I didn't know his name."

"I didn't get the impression they would be giving up any time soon. Brodie followed them back to town. They went straight to the bar and started doing some rabble-rousing. I'm almost surprised we haven't seen the torch and pitchfork crowd yet."

"The other man seemed like he knew you guys. He told the bald man—I mean Clint—that they'd end up worm food if they broke into your home."

Callum gave her a feral grin, and Wynne could have sworn his canines seemed larger than before. "The weasel's not as dumb as he looks. He's not wrong."

Her reaction must have shown on her face, because he immediately let his lips drop back into a neutral expression that hid his teeth. "Don't worry, though. You're not in any danger. We don't make a habit out of harming young women in need of sanctuary. Those idiots basically admitted that they chased you in here. And I don't believe for a second that their intentions were quite so honest as retrieving a stolen trinket. I could smell the lust on the big one."

Wynne shivered. Clint had started eyeing her the moment she walked into the village tavern three days ago. He hadn't taken it too well when she'd turned down his early advances. She'd seen that frightening glint in his eyes long before the supposed theft occurred. Clint didn't need another reason to chase her, but he'd take a plausible excuse.

"You know," he said as he stood. Now Wynne could really see how tall and broad he was. She felt her heart race as he invaded her space ever so slightly and was shocked to discover it wasn't fear racing through her veins. "If you told me what's going on, maybe I could help you."

"Maybe," she hedged, stepping away and turning her back to him. "But then again, maybe not." She risked a glance at him over her shoulder. "Besides, why would you want to? You don't know the first thing about me."

"I know you're cute when you snore."

Wynne felt her whole face heat and whipped her head around to stare at the wall. Stars above save her. She could only imagine what she must have looked like when they found her. Probably slack-jawed and drooling on this handsome man's pillow.

"Sorry," he chuckled. "Lightening the mood has never been one of my talents." He brushed past her on his way to the door. He turned back to her. "Anyway, judging by the amount of stew that was on the floor, I'm guessing you didn't get to eat much before the charm hit you. You must be starving. Let me make you a plate."

She wanted to say no, that she couldn't accept any more of their hospitality—even if most of it had been unwittingly—but her traitor stomach chose that moment to grumble audibly.

Callum gave another one of those honest, open laughs. "That's what I thought. Come on."

Soft lighting had transformed the front room of the cottage. A simple chandelier Wynne hadn't noticed before hung above the kitchen table with beeswax candles burning merrily in their holders. Oil lamps on either end of the mantle supplied a warm glow to the living space. It was a mild evening, and the hearth remained unlit.

"We didn't know for sure when you'd wake up, so we kept some dinner warm," Callum said, pulling a pan from the stove's oven. He gestured for her to sit at the table before plating what looked like a whole trout, roasted turnips, and spring salad on the forest green plate. "It's not fancy, but it should taste pretty good. I'm sorry there's no stew left. Brodie can be a bit of a hog."

Wynne's stomach rumbled again at the aroma of the food he placed before her. She was halfway through the pile of turnips when he plunked down the matching mug. One sniff told her it was a weak cider. Half the mug was gone before she knew what she was doing. She hadn't realized just how hungry and thirsty she really was.

"I don't know whether I should be insulted or flattered." Callum laughed. "I'm not sure you're even tasting those turnips."

"They're delicious," Wynne said before tucking in again. It was like the smell of food had temporarily erased her inhibitions. Right now, she was so hungry that the turnips could have tasted like dirt, and she would have inhaled them anyway.

"Just go slow with the trout. Wouldn't want you choking on any bones."

They sat in surprisingly companionable silence for a while whilst Wynne devoured both the turnips and the salad. When they were gone, she turned careful attention to the trout. It flaked beautifully under her fork, requiring scooping rather than stabbing. Flavor erupted on her tongue; fresh herb and garlic notes played with but didn't overwhelm the natural flavor of the trout. Wynne let out a small moan in spite of herself at that first bite.

Her host chuckled, of course. "It seems I haven't lost my touch with the trout."

"You made this?"

"All of it. Momma never got that daughter, remember? Somebody had to help in the kitchen."

"Thank you. This is very kind of you—especially after all the trouble I've caused."

"No trouble at all. Things could do with a little livening up around here."

Callum found he regretted those words almost as soon as they'd left his lips. Before his impromptu dinner guest had a chance to respond, the repaired front door flew open, and Alasdair's grim presence erupted from the darkness beyond.

"We've got company." His hazel gaze moved

to rest on Goldie. "Looks like your friends decided to make this a party."

Alasdair shut the door and moved into the living space. He spoke as he started moving furniture aside. "Brodie's going to try and talk some sense into them, but I doubt it'll be much use. Callum, I think it would be best if you take our guest somewhere a little less crowded." He whipped the rug aside to reveal the trapdoor to the cellar and their escape route.

Ever since the fire that destroyed their cub-hood home and claimed their father's life, the brothers had been prepared. There was no telling what petty conflict might turn neighbors into enemies, and three werebears were no match for a mob. Still, since the villagers weren't technically after them—yet—Callum hoped the house would survive this time. He grabbed Goldie by the arm. "Come on."

To his surprise, she didn't resist his gentle pull on her arm. Goldie followed him down the steep cellar steps with only a single oil lamp to light their way. He saw her flinch when Alasdair dropped the door shut over their heads. Footsteps and thumps followed as his brother rearranged the furniture to cover their departure.

"This way." Callum kept his voice low, but tried to keep his tone unconcerned, as if it were perfectly normal to flee in the middle of a late supper. "It may just look like a cellar, but I promise there's another way out."

"Why are you doing this?" she asked. "All

you would have to do is turn me over and they'd go away. Why take on so much trouble for my sake?"

"I told you, I could smell the lust on that bald idiot. I don't believe for a second he's telling the truth, and neither does Alasdair."

"What about Brodie?"

"He's out-voted."

"Are you always so democratic in your decisions?"

Callum looked back at her, flashing a smile. "No. Usually we just do what Alasdair says. Life's easier that way."

The entrance to the escape tunnel was hidden behind several barrels. The top halves were filled with useful things like dried fruit and nuts, but the bottoms were loaded with rocks. The idea was if the barrels were heavy enough, it would discourage anyone who did get into the cellar to snoop around from moving them. Callum wasn't thrilled to have to move them by himself now, but he was stronger than the average human. He scooted one of the barrels aside, revealing a dark hole from the floor to about waist height.

"Take this." He handed her the lamp and gestured to the hole. "Ladies first."

Callum expected an argument, but Goldie just clambered through the hole without comment. He followed behind, doing his best to pull the barrel partway back into place. His back was going to feel this tomorrow, he was sure.

Inside the tunnel, the ceiling was tall enough to allow them to stand. Pegs driven into the wall held three packs and wool cloaks. A tin lantern sat on the floor. Like the tunnel itself, Alasdair had been determined they would have everything they needed for a hasty exit should they ever need it. The packs were regularly refreshed with good rations and fresh waterskins. Their contents were rotated by season. Right now, they were still packed for chilly nights, what with spring just getting underway. Callum took his bag and forest green cloak down. He stuffed the cloak in the pack, then swung it onto his back with practiced ease. He paused to frown at Goldie.

"Did you have a bag somewhere? Any belongings?"

She shook her head. "Not with me. All my things are still back in the village. There wasn't time to grab them, and they would've just slowed me down." She shrugged. "Nothing I can't replace. I had my money on me, at least."

Callum pulled the cloak back out of his pack. "It may yet get chilly tonight. Spring around here is unpredictable. Plus, the hood will hide your identity if we run into anyone."

"What about you?"

"I run hot. I'll be fine. Here, is this too heavy for you to carry?" He handed her Brodie's bag. She hefted it experimentally, then swung it onto her back. "Good. Let's get out of here."

In which Goldilocks meets a Bear

The tunnel seemed to go on forever. Wynne stayed close to Callum and the lantern he carried. They'd left the fragile, blown-glass oil lamp behind. Somehow, the small portion of the tunnel that the lantern illuminated felt more claustrophobic for it. Dirt to her left. Dirt to her right. Above and below. They could only move forward. The air was cool, damp and stale—how she imagined a grave would smell, sans a dead body. Wynne swallowed against her panic. She was not made for this; she was made for open skies and grass between her toes.

"It's not much further," Callum promised.

"That's what you said an hour ago."

"We haven't even been down here for an hour."

"Could've fooled me," she muttered. It didn't surprise her when that made him chuckle.

"It's just the dark playing tricks on you. There isn't an hour's worth of tunnel unless you move at a snail's pace."

They walked on in a silence that was anything but companionable. The only sounds were their breathing and the mournful creak of the lantern dangling from its handle. Wynne hugged herself, struggling to keep her breathing even. She nearly jumped out of her skin when at long last Callum's voice broke the tense quiet.

"So, you want to tell me what this is about yet?"

"I told you, it's complicated."

He looked back at her over his shoulder. The lantern light cast menacing shadows across his features, but his voice was gentle when he said, "It seems to me that we have plenty of time for complicated stories. We still have a long walk ahead of us."

"I thought you said there wasn't an hour's worth of tunnel?" The high, panicked quality of her own voice frustrated her.

"Not all of our walk is underground," he assured her. "Unless you want to stop for the night a stone's throw from the village?"

Wynne shook her head, but before she could form an intelligible response, their dim circle of light illuminated a dirt wall and ladder.

"See?" he said. "That wasn't so bad, was it?"

"I'll tell you when we get out of here."

Callum shook his head. "Stand here and grab a hold of the side rail," he said, using his free hand to usher her to one side of the ladder. "I'm going to extinguish the lantern and go up for a look. If the coast is clear, I'll call you up."

"Do you..." Wynne swallowed convulsively,

struggling to form the words. "Do you really have to put out the light?" She hated the edge of hysteria that colored her tone. She squirmed under the intensity of his studying gaze.

"Are you afraid of the dark, Goldie?"

Wynne had to bite her tongue to keep from correcting him. It must have shown in her expression because a little half-smirk quirked up one corner of his mouth. *All you have to do is tell me and I won't call you that anymore,* it said.

"I don't do well with the dark," she admitted. Of all her secrets and fears, this was the one that would do her the least harm. He'd already guessed it, so she wasn't really giving anything away in the admission. He didn't need to know about the captivity that created her fear of small, dark places.

Callum frowned at her, and then at the lantern. It was the sturdy sort with a wick and a metal bottom that held the oil, but it wasn't the sort with shielding to block the light. He could turn the wick down to dim the light, but that might still be enough to give them away. Wynne could practically see the gears turning in his head.

"I'll be fine," she said, trying to sound stronger than she felt.

"You don't sound fine."

Wynne swallowed and shook her head. "I don't have a choice. I have to be fine. A little darkness—" She suppressed a shudder. "—never killed anyone."

He was still frowning when the light went out.

Wynne stifled a gasp with one hand and clutched the ladder's side rail tightly with the other. She barely registered the sounds of Callum setting the lantern down but could feel him pass by in the darkness as he scrambled up the rungs.

A cool breeze caressed her face. Wynne tried to breathe it in. It should be a relief after the stale, musty air of the tunnel, but she found that her lungs didn't quite want to work right. It was as if the darkness was pressing on her. Constricting. Suffocating.

"It's alright, Goldie. You can come up." Callum's voice seemed distant, like it was coming from a long way away instead of a few feet above her head.

Wynne's only reply was a thin whimper. Some small, rational part of her brain tried to make her body move, but her fingers had gone numb on the ladder. She was vaguely aware of Callum's whispered curses and the creak of the ladder as his weight settled back down on the first rung.

When he passed by her this time, Wynne recoiled, a small scream starting in her throat. A warm, broad hand covered her mouth and most of her jaw, pressing her back into the damp earthen wall. She screamed against his palm, her hands tearing frantically at his fingers and wrist.

"Shh, Goldie. It's just me. You can't scream. Someone might still be out there. You have to climb the ladder."

She thrashed against him, and Callum cursed.

"This would be easier if I knew your

name," he groused, his voice coming from somewhere close by her ear. His hand left her mouth, and she got half a shriek out before that same hand cupped the back of her head and forced her face into his chest. A thick, warm arm wrapped around her, pressing her up against him.

"Shh," he soothed, despite the fact that she was pummeling every part of his body she could reach. He took it all in stride, mumbling gentle encouragements. The hand that held her head massaged her scalp. "Shh, you're alright. It's alright. The sooner you calm down and climb the ladder, the sooner we can both get out of here."

Eventually, the panic ran its course, and Wynne felt herself go limp. Exhausted. She was still terrified, but her body had run out of steam for torturing itself. Taking several slow breaths, she pushed gently on Callum's chest. He released her, and she sensed him take a step back in the darkness.

"I'm alright now," she said. Her voice was shaky but calm.

She felt around in the dark with one trembling hand in the direction she thought the ladder must be. At first her fingers grasped only air, and her heart jumped, threatening another attack. Before the terror overwhelmed her, the back of her hand collided with the side rail. Wynne scrambled awkwardly up the rungs.

The night air felt fresh and clean after the tomb-like tunnel and she gulped it up, sprawled in the cool grass in front of the trapdoor.

Callum had never seen someone respond so viscerally to extinguishing the lights. He studied the shaking form of the woman before him. Hardly any moonlight managed to filter its way through the dense clouds overhead, but even in his human form, Callum had excellent night vision.

"I don't want to rush you," he said, keeping his voice just above a whisper, "but we can't stay here. It's not safe. We could be discovered by the mob on their way home or —" He paused, unsure how much to say; he didn't want to scare her. Although the clouds were hiding it, Callum was fully aware of the moon's phase. It was full, which meant his friend Bleddyn wasn't quite himself tonight. "Let's just say that now isn't a good time to be in the woods and leave it at that."

As if on cue, the howl of a wolf split the quiet of the night. Callum cursed.

"No time. Listen, I'm going to do something a little strange, alright? I need you to stay calm and get on my back, okay? I have to carry you, because we need to move quick." He didn't wait for Goldie to respond. Callum closed his eyes and let go of that secret part of himself. The blurring magic of the shift washed over him, bringing with it a pleasant sort of tingling sensation. There was a slight pinch, and when he opened his eyes again, the dark of the night seemed lighter, the shapes around him crisper, sharper.

Goldie shrieked and scrambled backward. If Callum hadn't closed the trap door behind him, she would have taken a tumble back into the hole. She was sprawled back on her elbows, staring at him with wide, frightened eyes. Callum let out a huff that was an ursine version of a sigh and approached her slowly. Her hazel eyes snapped shut as his nose came within inches of hers.

Without putting too much thought into what he was doing or why, Callum gave her cheek a quick lick. He sat back then, giving her some breathing room. Her tears were salty on his tongue, and he suddenly wished he could kiss them all away.

Goldie opened her eyes and stared at him. Callum gave her his best bear imitation of a grin.

"You're not going to eat me?"

Callum rolled his eyes and gave her an exasperated huff in response. They didn't have time for this. Callum was quick over a short distance, but he wasn't sure he was quick enough to outrun Bleddyn on a full moon. The werewolf was no danger to him, but the same could not be said for Goldie when the curse was in control.

"And you want me to get on your back?"

He nodded, and she bit her lip. Callum could understand her hesitancy, but now was really not the time to—

The wolf howled again. Closer. There was something slightly unearthly in that howl that made Callum's hackles rise. Goldie must have felt it, too, because she quickly—and somewhat awkwardly—climbed onto Callum's back. Her dainty hands were capable of a surprisingly firm grip, and Callum winced as she yanked on the fur at his neck. Her knees and heels dug into his sides. Bears were not designed to carry passengers.

Hold on, he thought. *This is probably going to be a bumpy ride.*

Wynne hung on for dear life as the bear—Callum, she reminded herself—loped through the forest. It turned out that bears didn't make for the most comfortable ride with their cantering gait. They did, however, cover a lot of ground quickly.

But not quickly enough.

A lithe shape burst from the woods ahead to their right, blocking the path forward. Callum skidded to a stop. Wynne screeched and clung to him, desperate to stay on his back. A low growl emanated from the creature, and Callum's sides heaved as he let out a threatening *wuff* in response.

"What in stars' names is that?" It was a pointless question, considering her companion's lack of speaking ability. Still, Callum was on the large side for a bear, and this thing looked to be almost as tall. Wolves didn't get that big... did they?

Callum let out another aggravated *wuff* and clacked his teeth.

The monster charged with a howl. Callum reared up, dumping a startled Wynne. She hit the ground hard as the two great beasts collided. The wolf—it was definitely a wolf, Wynne saw now—snarled as it lunged for the bear's throat. Callum bellowed and swatted the snapping jaws away with a powerful paw. His claws raked a row of bloody lines into the side of the wolf's face.

Wynne forced herself to move. An ordinary wolf by itself would be no match for a bear of Callum's size, but this creature was anything but ordinary. She couldn't just sit in the middle of the forest path and wait for them to trample her in their titanic battle. She had to find a way to help Callum so they could get away.

There wasn't much moonlight to work with this far into the woods—even less off the path in the undergrowth—but Wynne searched frantically, nonetheless. Surely, there was a big stick here somewhere. There were always big sticks in the forest, right?

Behind her, Callum bellowed again, and the wolf let out a high-pitched yelp. For a heartbeat, she thought maybe Callum had won, but more snarls and bellows followed.

Her hand closed on a downed branch that was easily as thick as her forearm. She jerked it upright and stomped on the other end, snapping the branch in half and leaving her with a manageable club. Perfect.

Wynne nearly screamed when she reached the path. Callum was covered in dark patches that shone wetly in what moonlight penetrated the canopy. The wolf, by comparison, was hardly looking the worse for wear with only the single bloody patch where Callum had smacked him initially.

The two of them were now wholly absorbed in their battle. Neither seemed to notice the human dashing out of the woods with her silly stick. The wolf darted and danced, trying to wear down the larger, heavier bear.

"You can do this Wynne," she told herself. "Deep breaths." She rolled her shoulders and readjusted her grip on the makeshift club. It was now or never.

With a banshee scream and a running leap, Wynne dove into the fray, bringing the club down with all her strength on the back of the massive wolf's head. To her shock—and Callum's apparently—the creature went down with a yip and stopped moving. Wynne dropped the stick and stared, her eyes never leaving the wolf's prone form. She couldn't quite believe what she'd done.

"We've got to get out of here before he wakes up."

The sound of another human voice startled her, and Wynne looked up to see Callum stumbling towards her in his human guise. He was bloody and limping. His eyes, she noted with some horror, still shone in the moonlight like an animal's.

"What is that thing?" Wynne asked, still staring at the monster's motionless form.

Callum grimaced. "Werewolf. Well, sort of. He's not such a bad fellow, usually, but his curse does funny things to his head around the full moon. That little love tap you gave him won't keep him out long, so let's get going."

He shifted again before her eyes. Between

one heartbeat and the next, a bloodied bear stood where the injured man had been. Wynne shook off her shock—she didn't think she could get used to him doing that—and climbed on his back, trying to be mindful of his injuries. Before she was even really settled, he took off again, his gait made even more uncomfortable by a pronounced limp. After a while, Wynne buried her face in the fur of his neck, shivering when she heard the sound of a wolf's mournful cry in the distance.

In which there is only one bed

Bleddyn's cottage looked the same as it always did. Smelled the same, too. Callum wrinkled his nose against the strong scent of wolf shifter that permeated the place. A banked fire in the hearth lent just enough light that even Goldie ought to be able to maneuver without tripping over anything.

"Where are we?" she asked, eyeing the place. Her delicate nose was also wrinkled, and Callum wondered if Bleddyn's wolfy stench was strong enough even for her blunt senses. "It smells like a village shinty team in here."

Ah, just the normal funk of human male then.

"Bleddyn's place. He, uh, won't be home tonight and the villagers wouldn't think to look for you here." He tried to be casual about it, keeping his back to her while he built up the fire, but something in his tone must have tipped her off.

"Bleddyn wouldn't happen to be the wolf I

just brained with a big stick, would he?"

"He just might be at that."

"And you don't think he'll mind us breaking into his home while he's... indisposed?"

"I doubt he'll mind a bit. Bleddyn and I are friends."

Well, as much as Bleddyn is friends with anyone, Callum amended silently. The werewolf wasn't big on people, but he tolerated the neighboring bears. Callum couldn't imagine the pain Bleddyn's curse brought him. Unlike bears, who were normally solitary creatures, wolves were social animals, perhaps even more so than humans. To live in isolation the way Bleddyn did had to be killing the man slowly.

"Some friend," Goldie muttered. Louder, she said, "We should probably do something about those wounds. You're bleeding all over the place."

"I just need to clean up a bit and I'll be fine. I heal quick. Benefit of being a werebeast."

"I'm sure even a—whatever you are—"

"Werebear," he interrupted. "I'm a werebear."

"Right. Anyway, I'm sure even a *werebear,*" she put heavy emphasis on the word, "can get an infection as easily as the next creature."

Callum chuckled but decided to humor her. Besides, he wouldn't mind an excuse for those delicate looking fingers to be brushing over his bare skin.

"There should be a box with medical supplies in the kitchen, and I have some in my bag."

While she was occupied rooting through the clutter on Bleddyn's shelves, Callum lit the oil lamps and a couple of candles. There was at least one cut on his back that he had to admit would, in fact, heal quicker with stitches.

"I need this filled with water," Goldie demanded, pointing at a cast-iron pot by the fireplace. "It looks clean enough. Where's the water?"

"Pump's outside." He plucked the heavy pot from its spot with ease. "Stay here, I'll get it."

"You're hurt."

Callum laughed. "Perhaps, but I carried you all the way here and I can still fill this pot with water. Besides, on the off chance that Bleddyn does come home before dawn, I still stand a chance; you don't."

"He could have killed you," Goldie protested. Her concern for him was actually kind of adorable, and Callum had to resist the urge to laugh again. He didn't think she'd see the humor in that statement.

"Even when he's sane, Bleddyn couldn't kill me, even if he wanted to. I was trying not to hurt the poor bastard since he's currently out of his gourd. I took a few scrapes for my trouble, but eventually he would have decided that tangling with me wasn't worth getting to you."

"Still..."

"Goldie, the only reason he even engaged in that fight was because he could smell you. I'll be perfectly safe fetching some water, I promise."

She still didn't look convinced, but Callum slipped from the tiny cabin anyway. Once outside in the cool dark of the night, he let his bravado drop. He limped along to the water pump beside the house. Thankfully, the metal mechanics of the pump were the one thing Bleddyn seemed to keep maintained. The handle moved easily, cold water gushing forth from the spigot.

Inside, he found Goldie had already spread out everything she thought she'd need on the rickety dining table. She'd found clean bandage strips in his pack, along with a needle and thread. Bleddyn's box of medicinals, Callum noted with amusement, sat untouched on its shelf. Goldie had pulled the only stool in the single room cabin in front of the hearth.

Goldie took the pot from him without a word and hung it over the fire. She threw some of the bandages, the needle, and several lengths of thread into the water with a handful of some herb.

"You seem to know what you're doing. Are you a healer?"

"No, but I've picked up the basics." Her tone was sharp, and Callum was starting to recognize it as a signal that she considered the question to be prying. "Sit down. And... and take off your shirt."

Was that a blush on her pretty cheeks? The firelight could be deceiving, but Callum was pretty sure there was a healthy flush of pink across her face. An unexpected coil of desire curled in his belly, and Callum found himself turning away.

She just wants to dress your wounds, you great idiot bear, he told himself. *Nothing more. She doesn't even like you.*

He removed his bloodied, ruined shirt and sat on the stool, presenting his broad back to her.

She worked with brisk efficiency, touching him as little as humanly possible as she dabbed away blood and examined the wounds.

"There's a lot of dirt in this one," she muttered, poking at a nasty gash across his ribs. "I'm going to have to be a bit less gentle with it."

"I'll be fine, Goldie. Do what you have to do."

"It's Wynne."

Callum looked down at the top of her head that was between his upraised arm and his side. She was so intent on the wound she was examining he didn't think she'd even realized what she'd said.

"Wynne," he repeated, testing the name on his tongue.

Her hands froze.

"It's alright. I don't know why you don't want me to know your name, but I won't tell a soul if you don't want me to. I can keep calling you Goldie."

She resumed her ministrations with a small sigh. "It's alright. After all you've done for me this evening, I owe you at least that much."

"Since you're feeling so generous, do you mind telling me why the villagers would risk a moon-mad lycan to get to you—ow!"

Wynne flashed him a satisfied smirk and stood up. She fished the needle and thread from the boiling pot with a ladle, placing them on a plate.

"Let's just let these cool, and then the real

fun can begin."

In the end, only two of his wounds required stitching. The one on his ribs, and the deep one in his thigh that was causing his limp. They'd both blushed a fair amount when Wynne had demanded that he remove his trousers and let her examine the bite. Bleddyn—the mad bastard—had taken a good chunk out of Callum's hide.

Wynne was exhausted by the time she'd finished patching up her would-be hero. She was still fuming with herself for having so thoughtlessly told him her name. And yet, she had to admit, Callum had put himself through a lot of trouble on her account without even knowing why. Perhaps she could trust him with her truths.

And perhaps not.

To say that the werewolf's home was unkempt was an understatement. Although it was planked wood, the floor might as well have been dirt for all the care its owner had taken with it. A haphazard pile of unwashed dishes sat in a metal tub by the door, apparently awaiting the next time Bleddyn decided to haul it out to the water pump. Much of the room was dusty, as though he didn't use the cottage much. Maybe he didn't.

The most distressing part of the whole thing was that there was very clearly only one place to sleep, and the night's adventures had cancelled out Wynne's impromptu nap. Callum, who had looked exhausted from the moment she met him, now looked dead on his feet.

Which reminded her— "Why did you have a sleeping charm under your pillow?"

One strawberry-gold eyebrow raised questioningly, as if he were saying 'oh, but *you* can ask questions,' and for a moment Wynne thought he might not answer. Then he gave her a rueful smile and gestured for her to have a seat on the bed.

"I suppose we have time for a story, since I won't be getting much sleep anyway. When I was barely more than a cub, my brothers managed to incur the wrath of a nasty old witch by disrupting her nap. Being older and bigger than me, they were a lot faster, and when the old witch came hurtling out of her cottage, well... I was the only foolish bear cub still standing there."

"Wait, are you saying the witch cursed you?"

"I don't remember exactly what she said, but I don't think I'll forget the crazy look in her eyes for the rest of my life. I had nightmares about it for weeks. Which I suppose was really the start of the curse.

"At first, I just had a lot of bad dreams. More than was usual for a child my age at the time. I woke up screaming at least once a night. Momma and my brothers got sort of used to it, eventually. As I got older, the symptoms of the curse changed. I began to have trouble falling asleep in the first place, and when I did, my dreams still were disturbing."

"When's the last time you had a good night's rest?"

"I was twelve when she cursed me. I'm thirty-three. You do the math."

Twenty-one years. The man hadn't slept well in twenty-one years. How was he healthy, let alone sane?

"On the bright side, I suppose, the witch wanted me to suffer as long as possible and the curse seems to keep the lack of sleep from making me truly sick. I feel like shit, though, and I thought maybe a sleep charm could counter-act the curse, at least for one night. It'd be nice to get more than four hours of rest."

The absurdity of the whole thing almost made Wynne want to laugh. Almost. Who cursed a child to sleeplessness?

"What happened to the witch?"

"Oh, she died eventually. I had hoped my curse might die with her, but no dice."

Wynne bit her lip. She couldn't cure his curse, exactly. In truth, only an exceptionally strong witch—one with formal training—could do that. Still, if she walked a fine line with her gift, maybe she could give Callum some relief for a night or two, depending on how long they remained in each other's company. The question was, could she do it without revealing her secret?

"I'm not tired yet," she lied, popping up from her perch. "Why don't you at least try to get some rest. Curse or not, you've had a rough night and your body needs sleep."

He gave her a lopsided smile and moved towards the bed. Leaning down, he once again invaded her space ever so slightly, staring down at her. There were only inches between his lips and her upturned face. Wynne's breath hitched. He wasn't thinking about what she thought he was thinking about, was he?

"Thank you, Wynne," he said at last. His eyes definitely darted to her mouth before coming back up to her eyes. "For listening, and for patching me up. I was a bit more banged up than I wanted to admit."

She couldn't stop herself from smirking. "So I noticed."

Wynne busied herself with cleaning up from her meager attempts at doctoring. She tried not to think too hard about what it had been like to touch his warm, golden skin but her hormones had other ideas. What it would be like to trace the trail of auburn curls that disappeared under his drawers—she shut that thought down. That was wholly inappropriate.

Callum tossed and turned on the bed, and she had to bite her tongue to resist the urge to scold him. He shouldn't be moving around so much with fresh stitches in his side and his thigh, but she needed him to fall asleep if she was going to try to do anything about the curse that kept him from staying that way.

Eventually, his breathing became deep and even. Wynne crept towards the bed, wondering if the curse also made him a light sleeper. The floorboards creaked under her feet, and she winced, but Callum didn't stir. He was lying on his back on the narrow bed —it was more of a cot, really—which didn't leave much room for Wynne to sit. She perched on the edge near his head and studied him.

His face had relaxed, making his features even more boyish. At least ten of his thirty years seemed to slough away in his sleep. Hesitantly, Wynne reached out and brushed a lock of sun-kissed auburn hair from his forehead. He hummed a bit, and Wynne wondered if that was a sound of contentment. Was it a bear thing?

Here goes nothing, she thought.

Carefully, slowly, Wynne opened the channels of her gift. Instantly, she could feel two powers swirling inside Callum. Her vision shifted, and then she could see them, like tendrils of smoke and light coiling through his body as if it were a vessel of glass. She poked at them, feeling the texture of them. The light was his shifter gift, an intrinsic part of him. If she were to yank on that, he would jerk awake from the pain of it. Having a born gift—a slice of your life's essence—siphoned out was excruciating.

The smoke, on the other hand, was not a part of Callum. Not really. When Wynne connected with it, the acrid taste of dark magic hit the back of her tongue, making her want to gag. This was the curse then. Siphoning this shouldn't hurt in the least. In fact, she expected that Callum would feel lighter than he had in decades.

Wynne took a sharp inhale of breath, and with it her magic began to suck out the curse. She watched in fascinated horror as the smokey tendrils were suddenly slurped in the direction of her gift's channels. It was horrifying, watching that dark magic rush into her own body, even though she knew it couldn't hurt her.

Siphons could steal the magic from another person, but they couldn't use it. While she carried the curse, it couldn't affect anyone or anything. Still, she could feel the evil taint of it, and it brought tears to her eyes because she knew she was going to have to put it back. Siphons could only hold on to another's magic for so long before they had to release it into another host, or in this case, back to its origin.

When it was done, Wynne slumped back against the wall at the head of the bed. She felt vaguely nauseous and imagined she could feel the curse coiling up inside her like a serpent. It was a figment of her imagination, of course. Any power she siphoned was contained in a special place inside her soul, safely away from her physical body, and that place was impenetrable unless she opened it for siphoning. There was no way the curse could taint her.

Gently, Wynne brushed the hair from Callum's brow again. If her hand lingered in his hair a bit longer than necessary, who would know?

"Sleep well, Callum," she whispered, her own consciousness going fuzzy around the edges. "You've more than earned it."

In which Goldilocks meets the Big Bad Wolf

Callum came awake slowly, which was strange enough in and of itself. The first thing he noticed was that his right leg hurt like hell. The second thing he noticed was that he most certainly was not in his own bed. Whatever his head was resting on was a lot firmer than his pillow and it didn't smell like bear or man at all. It smelled... feminine.

He cracked his eyes open—they were crusted with sleep for once—and found himself staring at a hand. That hand and his head were both occupying someone's lap. Sunlight seeped into the room around ill-fitting shutters.

The events of the night before slowly filtered through his sleep-addled memory. Their unexpected guests. The fight with Bleddyn. His sleeping charm.

The sleeping charm! It must have still had some juice left. His right hand—the one he wasn't lying on—flew to his shirt pocket, only to find he was bare-chested. He peeked over Wynne to see his shirt hanging by the dead fire, presumably to dry.

If it wasn't the sleeping charm, what then?

Wynne murmured in her sleep and shifted beneath him. Her right hand was on his head, and she stroked his hair a moment before going still again, her breathing still deep and even. He remembered telling her about the curse. Had she done something to combat his insomnia?

"Well, isn't this cozy? It's about time you woke up. I didn't think you were capable of sleeping so long, Baby Bear."

Callum groaned and pushed himself up into a seated position, disturbing Wynne. He was going to kill Brodie for calling him that in front of Bleddyn. The werewolf was standing at the foot of the bed, arms crossed over his chest, and one dark, winged eyebrow cocked. Three ragged streaks across his cheek were already healing. Callum had really only grazed him.

"What time is it?" Wynne groused, rubbing her eyes.

"About midday," Bleddyn answered, his eyes flicking to Wynne for a moment before settling back on Callum. He was trying to frown but couldn't quite hide the amusement coloring his voice. "Which one of you hit me upside the head? And don't tell me you didn't because I've got the goose egg to prove it."

"That would be Goldie," Callum said, remembering that he'd promised not to share her true name. "How about you make yourself useful and hand me my trousers?"

Callum watched her confused, sleepy expression morph into one of mounting horror as she looked first at him, then at Bleddyn, and back again. "I'll get them!" she volunteered, practically leaping from the bed as if she'd been burned. Callum tried not to let that sting his pride. That, and the way Bleddyn was now openly laughing at him.

"Here," she said, shoving the rough woolen garment at him. Two flags of red stained her cheeks. "I'll get your shirt."

"Um, do you think I could get a clean pair from my pack? There's a giant patch of dried blood on these."

"Oh, right. Sorry. Sorry!"

Wynne practically threw the pack at him and darted out the door, giving him privacy to get dressed. Callum wasn't sure why she bothered; it wasn't anything she hadn't seen the night before.

"How's your head?" he asked Bleddyn while shoving one foot down a leg of his clean trousers.

"Oh, it'll mend. It always does."

"Well, I can crack it again for you if you don't stop laughing at me."

The werewolf threw back his head and laughed harder.

Callum rolled his eyes and stood, pulling his trousers up and buttoning them in place. The stitches in his thigh and side pulled a bit. He should've had Wynne replace the poultices before getting dressed.

"Looks like I did a number on you last night," Bleddyn said, his tone suddenly serious. "I'm sorry about that, for what it's worth."

Callum waved the thought away.

"You can't help it. Besides, I'm only roughed up this bad because I was trying not to do permanent damage to your sorry hide."

"Well, I suppose the least I can do is provide some breakfast—or is it lunch?—for you and your lady friend. I'm assuming there's a story there," Bleddyn said airily.

"There might be, although damned if I know what it is," Callum said. "I'll take you up on the breakfast though. I'm starving."

Wynne found that she was having trouble reconciling this somewhat dashing man—Bleddyn—with the creature that had attacked them the night before. Except when he smiled; there was something decidedly wolfish about his lopsided grin. He had produced some venison steaks from stars only knew where and had proceeded to set up a sort of iron grill over the coals in the hearth. The steaks sizzled, and Wynne's mouth watered. The trout Callum had cooked for her seemed eons ago.

She and Callum sat side-by-side on the bed—not touching and maintaining at least three inches between their elbows—while Bleddyn occupied the home's only stool. It seemed the werewolf was not fond of company, or perhaps company was not fond of him. Either way, the seating arrangements were uncomfortably limited.

"So, how is it that you came to be running around with a delicious smelling human on the night of a full moon, Cal? I would have thought you of all people know better."

"It wasn't by choice." He gestured to Wynne with one thumb. "Goldie here pissed off the wrong person in the village. We had the whole torch and pitchfork routine show up on our front doorstep sometime after midnight. Likely, old Al kicked them out of the tavern to close for the night, and they were liquored up enough to follow the rabble rousers out to the cottage."

"Now that's interesting." Bleddyn's eyes—a pale amber that Wynne found unnerving—lifted from the steaks he was grilling to stare at her. "You must have *really* pissed them off. Usually, the humans don't leave the shelter of their little town on a full moon." He graced her with one of those wolfish grins again. "There's monsters about, you know."

Wynne felt the color rise in her cheeks. She'd done more blushing around these two men in the last twenty-four hours than she'd done in most of her adult life.

"I'm not a witch and I'm not a thief," she said, her chin lifting defiantly.

"I never said you were, darling."

"And I am most certainly *not* your darling."

Stars, Wynne, she thought. *What is the matter with you? Stop antagonizing every man you meet before you antagonize the wrong one!*

Well, she'd already done that, now hadn't she? Clint wasn't going to give up on finding her now. Not when he knew—or at least suspected—what she was. Siphons were worth a lot on the black market, and he'd be wanting to make up the money he'd lost when she'd tricked him. She shuddered inwardly at the idea.

Something of her thoughts must have slipped into her expression, because Bleddyn had stopped grinning and Callum was now emanating deep concern so strongly she didn't even have to look at him to know it.

"Anyway, sorry we had to meet under such dire circumstance," Bleddyn said, changing the subject. "I prefer not to meet people when I'm... not myself."

A thought occurred to Wynne. "Why do you have to... change... on the full moon, but Callum seems to be completely in control of his... change?"

The two werebeasts exchanged a look. Callum made a gesture that seemed to say 'it's your story. Go on.'

"My situation isn't an intrinsic part of being a werebeast." Bleddyn kept his eyes on the steaks as he spoke. "It's a separate curse that is triggered by specific conditions. I met those conditions when I was thirteen. I don't remember much about it and what I do remember isn't pleasant."

"There's an awful lot of curses going on around here," Wynne observed, eliciting chuckles from both men.

"Brodie's only curse is loose lips, if it helps." The trio laughed at Callum's joke and the mood lightened just in time for Bleddyn to announce that the steaks were ready. He flipped them easily onto chipped plates and passed them around.

"Sorry, but I don't have much in the way of cutlery. I don't usually need it," Bleddyn said, his shrug nonchalant.

Wynne decided not to ask him to elaborate.

Callum handed her the small knife he kept on his belt before picking up his own steak with his fingers and ripping off a chunk with his teeth. Juice that was suspiciously red ran down his chin and Wynne wasn't sure if she wanted to be repulsed or lick it off for him. She shook her head. Where had *that* thought come from? She averted her eyes, turning her attention back to her own meal.

"Are you sure these are done?" she asked when she cut into her steak, and it bled all over the plate. "It seems a little... rare."

"I can throw it back on for you if you'd like," Bleddyn offered. He wasn't using any utensils either, Wynne noticed, despite having a knife at his disposal. He talked with his hands, and his steak dripped on the floor when he spoke.

"That's alright... I'll manage."

After breakfast, Callum asked Bleddyn to check the wound in his side. He would have preferred Wynne's tender ministrations, but suspected she wasn't as comfortable with that sort of intimacy—real or imagined—

while the werewolf was about. So, he suffered through Bleddyn's rough prods and pokes with something vaguely resembling good grace.

"I think you'd best leave these stitches in another day," Bleddyn said at last. "We heal fast, but not that fast, and I got you good. Especially your thigh."

Callum huffed. It was as he'd expected. "Let's get some fresh poultice and bandages on it then. I was hoping not to have to deal with it on the road, but it is what it is."

"On the road?" Bleddyn's dark eyebrows rose in surprise. "Where are you going, exactly?"

Wynne had gone outside to do whatever it was women did upon waking up for the day and Callum listened for a moment to make sure she was still busy at the water pump before answering. "Wherever it is that Goldie's planning to go. She's got men after her; it's not safe for her to travel alone."

"And this is your problem how, exactly?"

Callum opened his mouth to respond but quickly shut it when he realized he didn't have a good answer to his friend's question.

"Yeah, that's what I thought," Bleddyn said with an insufferable, knowing sort of chuckle that made Callum bristle. "You're thinking with the wrong head."

"I'm just helping someone in need, that's all." His tone was too defensive, even to his own ears.

"So, you're saying you'd help her even if she wasn't blonde and gorgeous with a nice arse?"

If Callum had been a wolf like Bleddyn, he probably would have growled. As it was, he fixed his friend with the most affronted glare he could muster. "Of course, I'd help her if she wasn't..." He trailed off, searching for words. *The most beautiful woman you've ever seen?* his brain supplied.

"Yeah, uh huh, I believe you. Whatever you say, Baby Bear."

Stars above save his brother because when Callum saw him next, he intended to beat that lazy bear's brains in for telling Bleddyn that nickname.

In which Baby Bear and Goldilocks start a journey

In the end, Wynne and Callum stayed one more night with Bleddyn. The men opted to shift into their beast forms and sleep under the stars, leaving the bed for Wynne. She knew she ought to be grateful, but if she was being honest, the bedding wasn't quite up to her standards. She'd much rather sleep outside with them in the fresh breeze than inside the decrepit, musty cabin. There would be plenty of time for that later, when she was alone on the road again. Besides, offending a host who could turn into an enormous wolf at will just seemed like a bad idea.

They set out in the morning just as the sun was coming up. Callum had insisted on accompanying her at least as far as the next village. Wynne knew she ought to protest—going with her put Callum in more danger than he realized—but she couldn't find the will to put up much of a fight. He was genuinely pleasant company, and Wynne rarely got much of that. Besides, she couldn't deny his concerns about Clint and his posse waiting for her along the forest roads. With Callum's help, Wynne could cut through the denser forest interior without risk of getting lost.

"Not only do bears have an excellent sense of direction," Callum told her when she expressed her doubts about that claim, "but we can also smell when we've been somewhere before. Trust me, you won't go in any circles while I'm with you."

Bleddyn walked with them as far as the border of what he considered his territory. He strolled along, chatting amicably about nothing and everything until he reached some invisible line only he—and maybe Callum—could detect. Abruptly, he bid them farewell and shifted, sauntering off to their right. His dark gray and brown coat quickly fell out of sight amongst the thick brush.

"What's he doing?" Wynne asked Callum once the wolf was out of earshot. At least, she thought that he must be.

"Probably scent marking."

"You mean...?"

"Pissing on trees?" He glanced back at her to see her response, a small grin playing at his lips. "Yeah, pretty much."

The two of them followed what Wynne assumed must be a deer trail. It was narrow and winding, and she had to watch where she was putting her feet because rocks and roots seemed to reach up to trip her at every turn. Here and there, low hanging tree branches or tall shrubs would drape across the path, snagging her hair and clothes if she wasn't careful. Callum forged ahead as if none of it bothered him, and he knew exactly where he was going.

"How's your leg?" Wynne asked around midday.

"A bit sore," he admitted. Bleddyn had removed the stitches early that morning. Wynne was still shaken by the werebeasts' uncanny rate of healing. The scratches Callum had inflicted on Bleddyn's face had completely disappeared by the previous evening.

"Do you need to rest?"

He flashed her a smile over his shoulder that was almost as wolfish as Bleddyn's rakish grins. "Why? You need a break, Goldie?"

Wynne was used to traveling, but that traveling was usually on wide—if a bit rutted —roads, and often by cart when she could beg or buy a ride. This trudging through the woods thing was a new experience, and she was getting a little tired. Not that she'd ever admit it with Callum grinning at her like that.

"Actually," Callum said, coming to a halt, "I know the perfect place to stop for lunch that's not far from here."

They trekked on for what seemed like an eternity. Wynne was just about to ask him what his definition of "far" was when Callum made a turn to the right, stomping through the underbrush.

"There's another deer trail up ahead that crosses this one, but the meadow starts here," he explained, pushing aside the limbs of a ranging shrub. Bright sunlight, previously muted by all the green growth, rolled over Wynne like a warm blanket. She eagerly scrambled through the brush towards the promise of thick, lush grasses and open sky.

It was still early in the spring, but the meadow was already strewn with golden dandelions. Above them, the sky was not quite cloudless, with thick cumulus tufts floating lazily by. It was the perfect place for a picnic.

"Are you sure it's safe to just lallygag here?" Wynne asked as Callum dropped his pack in the grass.

"I doubt very seriously any of your pursuers would be lurking around this deep into the forest. Clint didn't exactly strike me as the woodsy type. Besides, I'd smell them long before they spotted us."

"Really?" She wondered just how good his sense of smell was. Bears were known for following their noses, but did that include werebears? The question must have shown in her expression, because Callum laughed and answered as though she'd spoken aloud.

"Really. My senses are duller when I'm in this form, but they're still a hell of a lot sharper than yours. We should be able to while away an hour here safe enough."

Their meal was a sad shadow of the picnic lunch Wynne imagined. Callum didn't bother to spread out a blanket. He merely handed her a waterskin and hunk of cheese before producing two slightly withered looking apples from his pack.

"We'll have something a bit tastier for dinner," he promised.

They ate in companionable silence, although the meadow itself was anything but quiet. Birdsong filled the warm spring air, and the trees rustled in a gentle breeze. It was almost... romantic. If she were prone to fanciful notions, Wynne could almost pretend that she and Callum weren't fleeing from men who wanted her dead or worse, and that this was really a picnic—or an illicit little spring rendezvous.

What would it be like? she wondered, glancing over at Callum. He was reclining, watching the clouds drift by as he took leisurely bites from his apple. What would it be like if she just leaned over and licked that trickle of juice from his chin? What would his kiss taste like? Winter apples and—?

Wynne shook the thoughts from her head. She felt flushed, and her heart was beating double time. What was *wrong* with her? This was the second time she'd caught herself daydreaming about licking food juices off his face. Admittedly, it was a gorgeous, tempting face, but that was hardly an excuse.

Down girl, she told herself. *In a few days, he'll be just a memory.*

Callum did his best to ignore the fact that Wynne was lusting. He could smell it—a subtle shift in her scent that was pumping out pheromones. Since there were no other human males—or females, for that matter—in the vicinity, he felt fairly confident that lust was aimed at him, and that made ignoring it doubly difficult. As much as he wanted to sit up, take her face in his hands, and kiss her senseless, he had to restrain himself. If—when—he got to enjoy that particular delight, he wanted it to be after the danger had passed and Wynne felt safe. The last thing he wanted was for her to regret it later and feel he had taken advantage of her vulnerable state or her reliance upon him to get through the forest.

That didn't mean he couldn't tease her a bit though.

"What are you thinking about over there that's got you blushing so hard?" he asked, his gaze still pointedly focused on the clouds and not her. He had to resist the urge to chuckle at her sharp intake of breath. She probably didn't even realize she did it. From the corner of his eye, he could see that her cheeks were now well and truly scarlet.

"N-nothing," she stammered. Then, in a more controlled voice, she added, "I don't know what you're talking about."

Callum rolled onto his side, head propped up on one elbow so he could look at her properly. Twin flags of color still glowed under her freckles. He gave her his best smoldering stare. "I think you know exactly what I'm talking about."

"I am most certain that I don't." The rejoinder wasn't particularly witty, but it was prickly, and Callum decided he'd needled her enough.

He chuckled and sat up, gathering the remains of their meal—some cheese and a half-empty waterskin—to put back in his pack. He paused and sniffed the air as a large, gray cloud passed overhead.

"We should get going," he said, climbing to his feet and shouldering the pack. "I don't like the way the air smells. It's going to rain."

Wynne looked around somewhat wildly, her eyes scanning the sky, which was still mostly dotted by fluffy marshmallow clouds. The smell of ozone was getting stronger, and Callum knew they would soon be pushed out by towering thunderheads.

"I know a cave we can shelter in, but we have a lot of ground to cover to get there."

"What? Do you think I won't be able to keep up?"

"Honestly? No, but it's not your fault. I've never met a human who could outrun a bear."

The look she gave him was part glare, part pout, and part pure exasperation. The way her lower lip protruded ever so slightly didn't match the glower in her eyes. It was adorable, but he had a feeling she wouldn't appreciate the sentiment any more than she liked hearing how cute her snores were.

"Let me put it to you this way. Which would you prefer: a short ride bear back, or a long walk in the rain?"

Wynne folded her arms and narrowed her eyes. "A pun, really?"

Callum sighed, shouldered his pack, and started across the meadow.

"Where are you going?" Wynne grabbed her own bag and jogged to catch up.

"Trying to get as close to shelter as I can before the rain starts pouring down on our heads."

She worried her lower lip between her teeth, and Callum had to suppress a groan. If she didn't stop doing that, he was going to break his promise to himself about trying to steal a kiss—the rain be damned.

"Do you promise not to throw me off again?"

He blinked. That's what was bothering her? "Well, I don't expect to be fighting off any werewolves this time, so I think you ought to be safe."

"Fine. But if you do, just know I'll never get on your back again."

Callum shifted, and Wynne jumped back with a yelp.

"I will never get used to that." She cocked her head to one side, studying him. "Where do your clothes and pack go?"

He huffed and lay down in the tall grass. Maybe she'd pull his fur less while getting on his back if he made it less of a climb. Wynne took it for the signal it was and made sure her pack was secure on her own back before climbing onto his. Callum rose, and she squeaked, burying her face and hands in the fur around his neck.

He set off at an easy pace compared to their harrowing flight the night before last. It was still faster than he suspected Wynne would have been comfortable walking. He knew he'd have to pick up the pace if he wanted to beat the storm, but he didn't want to scare her. Gray clouds were already starting to crowd the sun, turning the day from bright to overcast in minutes.

Wynne clung to Callum's back, her face still buried in the back of his neck. It was warm and surprisingly comforting. He smelled a bit like the meadow, like fresh grass and clover. She even caught herself holding on with only one hand and stroking the soft reddish fur. Hopefully, he hadn't noticed that.

Now that they weren't running for their lives, it was actually kind of thrilling to be riding on the back of a giant bear. How many women could claim to have done *that*? It was almost fun, as long as she didn't try to look at where they were going.

Thunder rumbled in the distance, and Wynne thought she felt the first drops of rain splatter the back of her head. It seemed like they weren't going to make it to shelter before the storm hit them after all. More drops followed those first few sprinkles, quickly building into sheets.

Callum pitched forward. For one terrifying second, Wynne found herself airborne. She barely threw out her hands in time to stop her face from colliding with the forest floor. The skin of her forearms shredded against the dirt, rocks, and roots. Behind her, Callum was making horrible noises—ursine moans of pain and fear. Shock held her immobile for what felt like an eternity before she was ablc to push herself onto all fours.

Several yards behind where Wynne had landed, Callum was standing like a statue, his sides heaving. His moans had turned to heavy huffs, but his eyes were wide with pain and outrage. Just above his right paw, blood was already beginning to run down the steel jaws clamped around his foreleg. Wynne scrambled to him, half crawling and running. The rain had started in earnest now, and the path was softening into mud. She brushed away the leaf litter concealing the bear trap. Her fingers came away sticky with blood.

"I don't know how these work." She didn't like the panic in her own voice, and she really didn't like the pain in Callum's eyes. "Can you shift back and help me figure this out?"

He shook his head in a very un-bearlike gesture.

"What do you mean, no?" Her voice grew shriller with every syllable. "Callum, I don't know how to help you. You're going to have to tell me what to do!"

Another low, rumbly moan was his only answer.

"Stay right here, I'll be right back."

Realizing what she'd said, Wynne cursed her own stupidity and darted away. *Where do you think he's going to go, you star-burned idiot?* Behind her, Callum bellowed. *I'm not leaving you, I promise,* she thought. *Just hold on, I'll be right back.*

For the second time in as many days, Wynne found herself searching in the forest for a big stick. It would have to be something good and stout if she had any hope or prayer of prying that thing open. Unfortunately, luck did not seem to be on her side. Despite having better light than the night she'd brained Bleddyn with a tree branch, Wynne didn't see anything nearly as hardy. As the elevation had risen, they'd entered an area dominated by evergreens. Most of the deadwood littered around her was the flimsy fan-like branches of pines and spruces.

Eventually, she found a long stick that was at least an inch thick and as long as her arm. It wasn't exactly straight, and she wasn't sure how much that would impact its effectiveness as a pry-bar, but it was what she had. Wynne darted back to the deer trail, slipping and sliding on the thick blanket of pine needles made slick by the rain.

She fell, landing hard on her knees. Her palms stung from the impact, and she had to pull pine needles from her hands. They were scraped and bleeding, but she'd live. Wynne couldn't say the same for her stick. It had snapped in half when she caught herself. Cursing, she made her way back to the trail anyway. Traps meant hunters. What if a hunter came by and brained Callum with a club while she was dillydallying in the woods looking for sticks?

By the time Wynne got back to Callum, she was completely soaked through and the front of her dress was covered in mud. Her breaths were coming in short huffs. She collapsed onto her sore knees in front of him and jammed the stick into the trap next to his paw.

"Come on." She grunted, pulling the stick towards her as hard as she could. The jaws of the trap didn't appear to be moving. "Come on, come on."

The stick snapped, sending her flailing back into the mud. Callum made another one of his ursine moans. He brought his free paw down on one side of the trap, batting at it insistently. Wynne hadn't noticed anything about the steel monstrosity before except the cruel teeth that were biting into Callum's flesh. Now she saw that there were two protrusions to either side of the closed jaws, and when Callum pressed on one of them, the jaws shifted.

Wynne quickly put a hand on each spring and pressed down. The jaws loosened, but not enough for Callum to free himself. She wasn't strong enough to reset the trap by herself.

"Callum, press down on the left side as hard as you can. I'll take the right."

Together they pressed the springs, and the trap sprung open. Instantly, Callum sat across from her, a man clutching a bleeding wrist to his chest.

"That doesn't count." He ground the words out around gritted teeth. "I didn't throw you on purpose."

Wynne laughed because if she didn't, she just might cry.

In which the Villain makes plans

She couldn't have just disappeared! The girl's a siphon, not a ghost!"

Clint winced when his boss brought his mug down on the table hard enough to shatter it. Outside, the thunder seemed to roar back in response. There weren't many things in the world that could make the battle-scarred thug wince, but the boss's temper was one of them. Ainsley Crichton, Lord of Windholt, was not a man to be crossed. Ale dripped from the table to puddle on the floor next to Ainsley's polished black boots.

They were in the back room of the tavern where Clint allegedly worked. As a wealthy visitor, Windholt had demanded the space for his private meeting room. He was here on business, after all. What exactly the villagers thought that business was, Clint wasn't sure. There was no one in the tiny village of Snoaksly-on-Barnham to do real business with.

"I'm telling you, boss, the girl is gone. She

didn't show up in Bowkerston, and she couldn't have made it to Heaversville already on foot. We've watched the cabin and the roads for two days now, and Jorge got hisself mauled out there."

"Did it ever occur to you that there's more earth to walk on than just the roads?"

Clint dared to laugh. "If she went into the forest that night, she's dead, boss. Everyone knows you don't go into Cumbersnatch Forest on the full moon."

"Do you even *understand* what a trained siphon can do?" Windholt's eyes were fever bright. It happened whenever he spoke of the siphons. "Even if your supposed crazed werewolf exists, she could suck the moon madness and shifter magic right out of him with the mere brush of a finger!"

"If she was trained." Clint echoed the man's own words back to him. "I thought you said this girl was clumsy at best."

Windholt ignored that. "Look here," he said, jabbing a finger on the map laid out across the table. The spreading pool of ale had started to seep into its bottom right corner. "This village is directly across the forest from here. If they head through the heart of the forest, they're sure to end up here."

Clint glanced at the town he was indicating. Wickersburg was a sizable town that sat on a profitable—and busy—trade road. If their quarry got that far, she could hop a cart to anywhere and be lost. "You think she would head straight for Wickersburg, through dangerous wildness?"

"Siphons will do anything—*anything*—to avoid captivity."

The bitch has a lot more to worry about than captivity if I ever get my hands on her, Clint thought. He indulged in a momentary fantasy in which the girl's pretty face was screwed up in a delicious expression of pain. He could almost taste her fear. But he had to snap himself back to the present, because Windholt was still talking.

"Take a few men and head to Wickersburg. You should be able to travel faster on the main road than what the girl can manage over rough terrain. Wait her out at least a week when you get there."

Clint grunted his acknowledgement. These weren't the worst orders Windholt had ever given him. An entire week in Wickersburg where there was a real whorehouse? That would do nicely. He could pack up tonight and head out at first light. The storm should be dissipated by then.

"And Clint," Windholt called, just as the big man was about to make his exit.

Clint stopped in the doorway and turned to look at him. "What?"

"I expect you to leave tonight."

In which there is no firewood

The remaining trek to the cave was blessedly brief, and Wynne nearly cried with relief when she saw its dark maw. She supposed that was why the hunters had set their trap along that path; a bear's cave must equal bear. The thought stopped her in her tracks.

"Callum!" She had to shout to be heard over the driving rain. "What if there's another bear in there?"

"Doubtful," he hollered back. "The place positively reeks of Brodie. He likes to camp out here from time to time when he can escape Alasdair. He'll disappear up here for a week at a time. Alasdair pretends not to know anything about it."

Somewhat reassured, Wynne put on a last burst of speed and sprinted to the cave with Callum hot on her heels. Ducking into the sheltered space was a relief.

The bottom of the cave had been dug out and made smooth, and Wynne found she could stand easily, although Callum had to stoop.

"Let me see your wrist," she said, tossing her pack aside.

Callum held the tender limb to his chest. "We have more important things to do. You're soaked and shivering. You can worry about my wrist after we get a fire going."

"I am n-not shivering."

He rolled his eyes. "Your teeth are literally chattering. Listen, we've gained a lot of elevation. Winter lingers a bit longer up in the hills."

Wynne tried to resist the tremors in her jaw but found she couldn't. Now that he'd pointed out her teeth chattering, she couldn't seem to stop it.

"Fine. You win. Fire first. But *I'll* do it. You just keep pressure on that wound."

He gave her a wan smile and gestured towards the back of the cave. "There should be firewood in here, if Brodie bothered to restock it. And a dry blanket. I'm afraid everything in our packs is as soaked as we are."

Wynne dumped her sodden cloak near the entrance before moving cautiously in the direction Callum had indicated. It was dark inside the cave, the only illumination provided by the feeble gray light creeping in from the entrance. Her feet and fingers both searched for a box or pile of wood. The promised blanket was there, along with what appeared to be a thin straw mattress. But no firewood.

"I don't think your brother restocked after his last visit," she said.

Callum swore. "Stars save that lazy bastard;

I'm going to break his nose when I get home."

"What are we going to do? There's no way there's any dry wood out there." She gestured helplessly at the gusting rain just beyond the cave's mouth.

"What we have to. We're going to get out of these wet clothes, do something about this." He held up his bleeding wrist. "And stay as warm as we can with the blanket."

If she'd had any heat left in her body, Wynne was sure her cheeks would have felt on fire. She understood the sense in what he was saying, but the idea of huddling naked under a blanket intended for one with a masculine specimen such as Callum was far more appealing than it should've been.

Well, she thought. *You wanted to know what his bare skin would feel like. Here's your chance.*

Callum's jaw dropped open of its own accord when Wynne loosened the laces on the sides of her kirtle and shucked it off. She gathered up her chemise and whipped it over her head in a quick, jerky motion. Her defiant hazel eyes met his, challenging him to look his fill, and his mouth went dry.

By all the stars in heaven, she was the most beautiful thing he'd ever seen. While her arms and face were sun-kissed and freckled, the rest of her was a perfect milky cream. Her breasts were more generous than her firmly laced kirtle had let on. Rosebud pink nipples puckered in the cold, and he almost forgot about the pain in his wrist.

"What? Did you expect more resistance? I can see sense once in a while. Or have you never seen a woman naked before?"

The barb shook him from his stupor. "I'm no untried boy," he growled.

She smirked. "Good for you. Now, hurry up and get undressed because I'm cold and you're still bleeding."

"This may be a bad time to mention it, but... I'm going to need some help. I think my wrist is broken."

Wynne uttered some very unladylike curses that would make sailors blush and stomped towards him, her waterlogged boots sloshing the whole way across the cave. She reached for the laces that held the neck of his loose shirt closed and began picking the knots apart without preamble.

"What did you do to these laces?" she griped. "Oh, forget it."

Before Callum could even question her intentions, Wynne had grabbed the knife from his belt and sliced the laces of his shirt. Her fingers tugged at the laces of his trousers and Callum flushed. The proof of his less than appropriate thoughts was clearly on display, although the proximity of that knife was rapidly curing it.

"You'll need these more than the shirt. At least you tied them properly," She stuck the knife back in his belt, then began unbuckling it. It was tossed aside unceremoniously as she pulled his shirt loose from his waistband. "Alright, arms up, bend forward," she demanded.

Callum didn't think he'd ever been stripped with more brisk efficiency in his life. Certainly not by a gorgeous, naked woman. He wished she'd taken her time, perhaps even brushed some kisses against his heated skin as it was revealed.

But she didn't even give him time to fantasize about it. As soon as he was naked, Wynne turned away, her focus on their packs.

"Things are a bit damp," she said, riffling through a bag, "but I don't think anything's actually ruined." She pulled his blanket out and squeezed sections of it. "Most of this is wet, too, but I think I can cut a strip from this dry spot to wrap your wrist. It's not clean or ideal, but it'll be better than nothing."

Wynne pushed him toward the straw mattress and demanded he sit. Callum submitted to her ministrations, grinding his teeth against the pain while she positioned his wrist against his cooking spoon and bound it tight with the strips she'd cut from his blanket.

"There, that should do it," she announced. "I hope your werebear magic can set your bones properly as you heal, because I have no idea what I'm doing."

"I'm sure it'll be fine."

They stretched out awkwardly on the straw mattress, the blanket pulled up to their chins. Wynne seemed to be doing her best to prevent any of her skin coming into contact with his, despite the fact that the meager bed was hardly big enough for two people to begin with. He could feel the blanket shudder with each of her shivers.

"Damn it, Wynne," he said after far too many minutes of listening to the rain and staring at the back of her head. "You're still freezing. Scooch closer. I promise I'll keep my hands to myself."

What if I don't want you to keep your hands to yourself? Wynne thought.

All she had to do was turn over and kiss him and they could engage in a whole other method of getting warm. And why not? Didn't she deserve to have a little happiness now and then? Sex with Callum would make her very happy—for a little while.

"Wynne?"

"Fine." She wiggled backwards until the skin of her back brushed the curls on his chest. Her behind was grazing against something that she was doing her damnedest not to think about. A strong arm snaked over her waist, pulling her tight against that broad, *warm* chest.

"You're not cold at all," she accused.

"No, but you are."

Wynne settled back against his comforting heat. His splinted wrist and hand stayed a respectful distance away from any of the important bits, and that was disappointing. Callum was being as much of a gentleman as their circumstances would allow—and Wynne hated it. She squirmed against him, pressing against the proof that she wasn't the only one affected.

"Wynne." His voice was a growl, low and sexy. "If you don't stop that, we're going to have a problem."

"What if I want that problem?"

He chuckled, and her heart skipped a beat. Then his lips were brushing her ear. His hot breath tickled in all the right ways as he spoke. "When I make love to you for the first time, it's going to be in a bed, with all the oil lamps burning." He gave her earlobe a little nip that made her gasp. "Now go to sleep."

In which Goldilocks tells the truth

He must have dozed off because Callum woke up on his back with a head of golden hair resting on his chest. Wynne had also rolled over in her sleep, and was presently plastered to his side, one arm and one leg thrown over his body. She was snoring softly.

He stroked her hair with his good hand, relishing the sensation of holding her. It was strange, but ever since she'd waltzed into his life, his curse seemed nullified. He wouldn't have expected the old witch to include a true love clause, and besides... didn't those usually require a kiss or something?

Everything about Wynne seemed designed to draw him in, including the mystery of her. Callum liked puzzles, and the fact that Wynne came with one was almost as irresistible as her fragile smile. Knowing the attraction was mutual made his heart do a fluttery jig of anticipation. Keeping his hands to himself until they reached Wickersburg was going to be the death of him.

It was morning, and although the rain was still coming down outside, it seemed to be petering out. The worst of the storm had passed in the night. The air inside the cave was still chilly where his skin was exposed, but they were toasty warm under the blanket.

Perhaps too warm.

Callum shifted his hand from Wynne's hair to her forehead and nearly swore aloud. Her skin felt scalding. She must have caught something out in the rain, or perhaps in Bleddyn's filthy excuse for a house.

"Wynne." He spoke at a normal volume and shook her shoulder. "Wynne, honey, I need you to wake up."

She murmured a weak protest.

"Come on, Wynne. I really need you to wake up now, sweetheart."

He pressed a kiss to her forehead; it was scalding against his lips. Was the fever already bad enough to do permanent damage? Would it kill her? He didn't know enough about fevers. He had humored Wynne about his wounds because he knew they'd heal faster with attention, but infections just weren't something werebeasts had to deal with. Something about the nature of their magic protected them from such things.

Her body convulsed, and Callum sat up in a panic, pulling her up with him. She convulsed again, like she was dry heaving. He pulled her hair back in case she was somehow going to vomit in her sleep.

Wynne's eyes flew open, and Callum

yelped. The irises and pupils of her eyes were gone. It was like looking into glass marbles filled with dark smoke. She heaved forward, and a black substance poured out of her mouth.

"Wynne!"

Her head snapped in his direction, her sightless eyes directed straight at him. Her hand—which had been limp at her side—flew up to grasp his arm.

It felt like getting body-slammed by both his brothers at once, and yet he didn't go flying across the room from the force of the concussion. Callum's head spun, and for a moment he thought *he* might vomit. A familiar weariness settled around his neck like a millstone.

His curse.

Wynne went limp. Callum didn't know whether to gather her up in his arms or drop her like he'd been burned. He opted for the former, pulling her cooling body close, his unshaven cheek resting against the top of her head. She was almost back to a normal temperature.

So, that solved the mystery of where his curse had gone. Unfortunately, it left him with more questions than answers. He only prayed that Wynne would wake up soon and explain what the hell had just happened.

Wynne found her way to consciousness slowly. The channels of her gift burned. It was a nasty sensation, like threads of fire just under her skin that left a horrible itch in their place. A roiling in her stomach and a pounding behind her closed eyes were classic symptoms. Siphoning sickness.

Wynne squeezed her eyes tight against the ache in her head. When she opened them, she found herself staring at a ceiling of stone. Flickering light cast ominous shadows across the rough, gray surface. Her brain struggled to connect the dots.

"Callum?" His name on her lips was almost more of a groan. Her mouth felt like a desert.

He dropped whatever he was doing; she heard a clatter that sounded like wood striking the dirt floor. Footsteps rushed to her side, and she turned her head ever so slightly to look at him.

Relief flooded his haggard features. The copper stubble on his face had grown into the beginnings of a true beard and he looked exhausted. Guilt nearly overwhelmed her. She'd lost control of her gift, and his curse had rebounded on him horribly. His honey brown eyes scanned her face anxiously.

"Are you alright, Wynne?" he asked quietly.

"I will be. What about you?"

He grimaced. "Well, my curse is back, but I suspect you already knew that."

"I expect you have a lot of questions. Callum, I'm so sorry. I—" One warm, calloused finger pressed over her lips, silencing her self-recriminations and explanations.

"Will have plenty of time to explain when you're feeling better. You've been out cold for a day and a half, so I'm sure you're hungry. Do you think you can sit up?"

Wynne's stomach roiled at the thought of food, but she knew he was right. She also knew from experience that the longer she put off eating following an episode of siphoning sickness, the worse it would be. It had been years since the last time she'd made such a foolish mistake, but Wynne remembered it vividly. She shuddered, and Callum frowned.

To distract herself, she asked, "did you say we're going to have sex with the lamps burning?"

Callum barked a surprised laugh. "Geez, Wynne, you really have a one-track mind."

She did her best to give him a smile. "I think I'd like to sit up now, but I'm going to need your help."

He scooped her up, blanket and all, hauling her up against his chest. She pressed her face into the crook of his neck, inhaling deeply. On the surface he smelled of pine sap and woodsmoke.

It was only a few steps to the stone ring that contained the fire. Callum sat her down gently in a seated position where the smoke would bother her the least. To her surprise, he kissed her temple before releasing her and shuffling off to grab a waterskin and an apple from his pack. She accepted the waterskin gratefully. It was half-empty, but it still felt heavy to her, and Wynne's arms shook a little with the effort to lift it to her lips. Seeing her struggle, Callum gently lifted the end of it, helping her tip a small amount of liquid into her mouth. She swished it around a bit to wet all the nooks and crannies of her mouth before swallowing.

"Stars above, I hate siphoning sickness," she said after a few more sips. "That's enough for now."

To her surprise, Callum didn't press her for details. Instead, he sat next to her and began to slice the apple, handing her a piece to nibble on. Wynne forced herself to take a small bite of it, chewing it thoroughly before forcing herself to swallow. It settled in her stomach like a huge hunk of lead. It was an effort to finish that slice. For several long minutes, the only sounds were the crackle of the fire, the snick of Callum's knife as it bit through the stiff fruit, and the small sounds of Wynne's chewing. When the apple was half gone, she refused another piece.

"That's all my stomach can handle for now. I'll eat more in a bit, I promise."

Callum frowned but polished off the apple.

"You've asked me a few times what was going on, and I dodged your questions every time," she said, shifting self-consciously and staring into the flames. She could feel his eyes on her. Her naked body was completely hidden by the blanket, and yet she'd never felt so bare in all her life. "And last night—or the other night—what you saw must have been frightening." Her eyes lifted to meet his. "I wouldn't have blamed you if you left me here."

"Like hell I would," he growled. His expression was fierce, made harsh by the firelight. "We may not have known each other long, Wynne, but I would've thought you'd know me better than that."

"I know," she whispered. Then, louder, she said, "I've never lied to you but there's a lot I haven't told you. I meant it when I said helping me was dangerous. I exposed myself back in the village and now the hunters are after me. Do you know what a siphon is?"

His brow furrowed. "Some kind of fae creature. Steals other people's magic and uses it against them."

Wynne snorted. "Not exactly. Siphons are thought to be part fae, but since we're born seemingly at random in human bloodlines with no known fae connections, it's hard to say if fae blood is the cause. And yes, we can siphon magic from other people and creatures, but we can't use it."

"Then what do you do with it?"

"Usually transfer it to someone else. For example, I could siphon your curse out of you and into someone else if I so chose. In some cases, a siphon may store magic on another's behalf. We usually can't do this for very long without having something like an allergic reaction. It's called Siphoning Sickness, and when it happens, our souls expel whatever we're storing into the nearest viable receptacle. If we can't, we die of a sort of anaphylaxis."

She took a deep, steadying breath.

"I'm sorry, Callum. The first rule an ethical siphon follows is to never do so without permission. I siphoned your curse without asking. I thought I could bring you some relief for a day or two. I should have siphoned it back into you sooner and given my gift a chance to reset itself, but—" she paused for a long moment, tears forming in her eyes— "you seemed so much lighter without it, I couldn't bear to do it. And then I waited too long, and you had to suffer the consequences along with me."

Once she started sobbing, Wynne found she couldn't stop, her body curling in on itself.

"Hey, hey, hey," Callum said, gathering her into his arms. One hand stroked her hair while the other rubbed comforting circles on her back. "Shhh, it's okay. You were only trying to help."

Wynne didn't know how long they sat like that, her sobbing into his shirt while he murmured sweet comforts in her ear.

Eventually she pulled away, wiping at her cheeks. "Sorry."

"It's alright. So, you're a siphon. That still doesn't tell me why those men were after you."

"Are," she corrected. "You can bet they haven't given up yet. Siphons are worth a lot of money on the black market, willing or otherwise. Some siphons voluntarily sell their services to a powerful master who can offer them protection. Others are forced into using their gifts for all sorts of awful things. A free siphon is very rare and only stays that way if they're able to keep their mouth shut and their gift hidden. Idiots like me get caught."

"You're not an idiot," he said, surprising her by taking her hand in his.

His thumb brushed circles over the back of her hand. It was a small, comforting touch. Wynne wondered if he knew how much danger such a touch could be between a werebeast and a siphon. Did he trust her that implicitly, or was he ignorant of what she could do to him if she chose?

"Do you know what happens when a siphon takes the magic out of someone with an intrinsic gift, like a werebeast?"

The motion of his thumb stopped.

"It's agony, first of all, to have what is essentially part of your soul ripped out. And then you die; slowly and painfully. That's why people think we use their magic against them. In the absence of it, they waste away."

Callum was quiet for a long moment while he processed this new information. Then his hand tightened on hers for a second before he readjusted his grip, lacing their fingers together.

"You wouldn't do that to me. Or anyone else." He said the words with more conviction than Wynne had thought possible. She smiled and squeezed his hand in return.

"You're right, I wouldn't. But another siphon did. I encountered their victim in Heaversville a couple of weeks ago. When I realized what had happened to the girl, I knew I had to help. So we followed the trail, which lead us to Clint in Snoaksly-on-Barnham."

It was a rough trip to the little village. By the time they'd gotten there, the poor fae girl could hardly walk. Wynne still wasn't sure what the girl's gift was, but it didn't matter;

without it, she would die.

"We barely caught the siphon before he left town. It took some convincing,"—Wynne had held a knife to his throat and threatened to cut off his balls— "but eventually he told me what he'd done with the victim's gift. Then I sought Clint out at the tavern. He started in with the leering almost immediately. I was repulsed, of course, and rebuffed him in no uncertain terms."

"I'm sure he loved that."

She smiled in satisfaction at the memory. "In retrospect, dumping his ale over his head probably wasn't the wisest move, but it gave me an idea. I made nice with him later, offering him a fresh ale and some... recompense. He followed me back to my room willingly enough after downing the whole mug. I still can't believe the idiot didn't suspect anything was amiss. Thankfully, the drugs worked, and he passed out before he could do much more than grope me." She shuddered. "I siphoned the girl's magic back out of him and into its rightful owner. She left immediately after that. I don't know where she went. It's safer for her that way."

"But you weren't able to get out of town before Clint woke up."

"A miscalculation on my part. I thought he would be out cold for a few hours at least. I wanted to see what I could find out about who he was working with."

"And?"

"I'm not a very good spy."

Wynne winced and rubbed at her temples. All this talking so soon after her episode was making her head pound.

Callum's frown deepened. "I think that's enough story time for now," he announced. "Let's get some more food in you, and then you could do with some more rest."

Wynne's stomach still twisted at the thought of eating, but she smiled and nodded. When he handed her a hunk of hard cheese and some jerky, she did her best to force them down. Water helped. Then Callum lifted her gently and placed her back on the straw mattress, away from the smoke of the fire and the chill air at the cave's mouth.

"Will you join me?"

"I'm afraid I won't be the best bed fellow at the moment," he said. "Curse and all that."

Guilt tore at her. If she'd been more careful, if she'd managed her gift better—

"Hey. Whatever you're thinking about, stop it."

"Am I that obvious?"

"Yes. Scoot over."

She made room, and he stretched out on his back, allowing her to place her head on his chest. The warm, safe feeling of his embrace almost brought tears to her eyes again. How could he forgive her? Trust her? It was almost more than she could bear. There was so much more she wanted to tell him, to trust him with in return.

"Thank you, Callum."

In which Goldilocks is clumsy

If she was nervous about riding on his back again, Wynne didn't say anything. Callum was mildly concerned after the last two experiences, but Wynne was still incredibly weak, and they needed to get somewhere with proper food and beds. Third time seemed to be the charm though, because they made it through the first day without incident and camped by a little creek.

Callum had happily raided Brodie's stash of supplies in the cave to supplement their own, and it seemed their middle brother was more industrious than Callum and Alasdair gave him credit for. There was a lot of smoked meat and fish, pickled vegetables, and even nuts and dried fruit stashed away.

Among the supplies in their packs was a small iron cook pot with a tripod. Callum rinsed the pilfered salted venison in the creek before putting it in the pot with water and beans. His nose had served him well that day on their trek, and he was able to add some edible mushrooms and wild garlic to the pot. Before long, it was simmering, and the smell was making his mouth water.

"This is what I intended our first night in the woods to be like," he told Wynne as they sat by the fire after their meal. "I meant to give you a prime camping experience, not—whatever that was."

Wynne smiled, the warm firelight casting her features in gold and shadow. "It wasn't your fault." Something mischievous twinkled in her eyes for a moment. "And it wasn't *all* bad."

Callum felt like a weight had been lifted off his chest. She'd been quiet and withdrawn since waking after their discussion in the cave. He hadn't been sure if it was just her physical condition, or if it was something else. Just in case—

"Give me your hand."

Wynne froze for a second, but eventually slipped her slim fingers into his palm. Callum readjusted his grip, turning her hand over to expose her palm. He ran one finger over the most prominent crease. Wynne stifled a giggle, and he looked up.

"Ticklish?"

"A bit. What are you doing?"

"When we were little, my mother would tell us stories of the Witches' Wood. She said there were women there who could read your whole life story—from birth to death—in the palm of your hand."

"And you think you've suddenly been granted that gift?"

He waggled his eyebrows at her. "Perhaps."

Before she could pull away, he readjusted his grip again, so that they were truly holding hands, their fingers laced together.

"I'm not afraid to hold your hand, Wynne." He gave her hand a gentle squeeze as he spoke. "I want you to know that."

"You do realize that I could kill you with a single touch if I wanted to? You would be in too much pain to even retaliate. It would—"

"And yet I let you ride on my back with your arms around my neck all day," he interrupted. "I know what it could do to me, Wynne."

"No, you don't. You've never seen—"

"And I don't need to. I trust that you won't do that to me. That's not who you are. And that's why I'm not afraid to hold your hand— or give you bear back rides." He chuckled at his own double entendre.

They were quiet for a time. Wynne didn't pull her hand away like he'd expected. Instead, she leaned in and rested her head on his shoulder, her eyes staring into the flames. Callum let himself revel in the closeness, quietly breathing in her scent and observing all the little movements in her brow as she sorted out the thoughts swirling around behind it.

"My mother told me a story once," she said at long last. "Does your village have Star Readers?"

"Yes. Although people mostly consult them on the best time to plant, breed cows, that sort of thing. Occasionally a parent will request a reading after a child's birth, but most don't bother."

"Father had a Reader present for my birth. My parents were rather well to do at the time. Anyway, as soon as I was born, they had a reading performed. According to my mother, the Reader smiled and said I had the loveliest birth blessing he'd ever seen. He said I was destined to be well and truly loved."

She sighed and Callum tensed, anticipating a cruel twist. He didn't have long to wait.

"Apparently, it was the worst day of her life. I was a double disappointment; I was a girl, and there was no wealth for the family in my future." A bitter smile twisted Wynne's lips. "It's ironic, really."

She pulled away, shaking her head. A shiver passed through her, and Callum couldn't tell if it was from revulsion or the cold.

"Tell me about your family, Callum. Something happy. About your parents and your brothers. You must have a million stories."

"First, a blanket." He pulled one from his pack and wrapped it around her shoulders. "What would you like to know?"

In the end, he told her every story he could think of, from the funny to the just plain stupid. Wynne laughed with each tale, enjoying second hand the antics of the three unruly bear cubs. Eventually her eyelids began to droop, and she rested her head on his shoulder again without seeming to be aware of what she was doing. Callum put a tentative arm around her, lowering his voice as he finished the last story for the evening.

She sighed into his shoulder and her breathing deepened into sleep.

"Goodnight, Wynne," he whispered. "Sleep well."

With the curse heavy about him, sleep would not come soon nor last long, but tonight he found that he didn't mind it so much.

It was the scent of cinnamon that roused her. Wynne wasn't surprised that Callum already had breakfast started when she woke. Her stomach grumbled, enthused by the warm, delicious smells wafting from the fire. At least her appetite was back, even if her head still swam with the lingering effects of her illness. She groaned as she rolled into a seated position. Her whole body ached, especially her thighs and lower back. Had she slept on every root and rock in the forest?

"Good morning," Callum said, his tone surprisingly cheerful for a man who had barely slept. The telltale smudges had already started to form under his eyes again. Wynne felt a twinge of guilt. She had a lot of nerve to be disappointed with *her* quality of sleep.

"Good morning. What's for breakfast?"

"Oats and our last apple. Plus, a little pinch of something extra from Brodie's secret stash." He winked at her and passed a tin plate and spoon.

"Are you sure Brodie won't mind you swiping his supplies?"

"I'll replace anything I took. Besides, I look at it this way—this is the price for my silence. I *could* have ratted him out to Alasdair long before he figured it out. I *chose* not to."

Wynne laughed and took a bite of the oats. Of course, they were delicious, just like everything else Callum had made for her. She was actually starting to get a little jealous. Even with a proper stove and a fully stocked larder, Wynne didn't think she could come close to Callum's culinary talent.

They were quiet for a while, each lost in their own thoughts while they ate.

"I'd like to wash up a bit in the creek before we go, if that's alright," Wynne said at last. She felt herself flush a bit when Callum's gaze snapped up from his food to meet hers. "I can't do much about my clothes, but my body feels sticky and gross from all the post-fever sweat."

She was surprised by the color she saw creeping into his cheeks. Wynne was beginning to get the distinct impression that Callum had a stronger sense of propriety than she did. After all, *she* was the one who had brazenly stripped bare when he suggested they get out of their wet clothes. And she was the one who had come on to him.

Oh stars, I did do that, didn't I?

"It's nothing you haven't seen before," she reminded him with a little smirk. She wasn't sure who she was trying to fool, him or her.

There was as much heat in her cheeks now as his. Not to mention other places.

Callum cleared his throat and looked away. He quickly busied himself with cleaning up as he spoke. "I'll pack up camp while you bathe. Just stay close and holler if you need anything."

Wynne thought about teasing him some more, telling him not to peek, but thought better of it. She *wanted* him to peek, she realized. She had a sneaking suspicion that he wouldn't, though—even if she told him to.

Standing up was harder than Wynne expected. She hadn't hurt this much since the last time she'd been beaten for refusing to siphon a gift. Her stiff leg sort of locked, and she staggered.

Before she could quite tip over, Callum was there, one arm gently curled around her back and the other supporting her forearm. "Are you alright?"

"Yeah, just a little stiff. Nothing I can't walk off."

Callum eyed the water, then looked at her, frowning. "The creek's not very deep. Maybe you'd better sit in it."

She laughed. "If I get down in that chilly water I might not get back up."

"I'll help you," he mumbled, and she saw that damning pink hue steal over his cheekbones. Her stomach did a little flip and a hunger ignited in her that had nothing to do with breakfast.

Stars, Wynne. You can hardly walk and you're thinking about that? she scolded herself.

"Think of it as a trust exercise," Callum said, apparently misunderstanding the reason for her prolonged silence.

"Oh. Sure." Wynne looped her arm through his, allowing Callum to help her stumble through their little camp towards the creek. Then he stood with his eyes closed and his arms outstretched to take her clothing. Wynne shucked off her dress as best she could, occasionally grabbing Callum's arm to keep her balance. His silly attempts to preserve her modesty would have made her chuckle under better circumstances.

"Okay, I'm ready."

Callum wadded up her clothes and tucked them under one arm before holding out his hands for hers. With his eyes still closed, he helped her lower herself into a kneeling position in the gently flowing stream. Wynne shivered as the frigid water touched her skin, grateful for the warm sunshine that cascaded through a break in the trees.

She rinsed the dried sweat and a dirt from her body as quickly as she could. The scrapes on her arms from her impromptu dismount the other night were scabbed over, and she resisted the urge to pick at them. Callum's inhuman healing ability was as enviable as his cooking. One would never know he'd broken his wrist just a few short days ago.

Occasionally, Wynne glanced up at him, checking to see if he'd given in yet. His eyes remained firmly closed. In fact, Callum appeared to be squeezing them shut tighter with each passing minute. His nostrils flared as though he might be in pain.

"Alright, I'm done," she said, grabbing hold of his hands and pulling herself to standing again. Before she was fully upright, Callum stepped back, apparently intending to lead her out of the water. Wynne pitched forward with a squawk.

Apparently realizing his mistake, Callum surged forward, and Wynne's face smacked into his chest. She bounced off and would have landed on her arse in the creek had his arms not closed around her. They stared at each other with twin expressions of shock.

Wynne regained her composure first. "I told you it's nothing you haven't seen before."

Callum groaned and closed his eyes, although this time Wynne didn't think it had anything to do with her modesty. Before she could react, he'd swept her up into his arms, carrying her bridal style back to camp. He plopped her down on her feet and thrust her clothing at her, his eyes once again averted. She couldn't help but giggle at his strained expression.

"I'll be right back," he grunted. His shift from man to bear was complete almost as soon as the words left his mouth. Wynne smothered another giggle as the shaggy werebear barreled out of camp.

I haven't laughed this much in years, she thought, pulling the dirty chemise on over her head. She stared at the place Callum had disappeared into the underbrush as she pulled on her stained and tattered frock. The future cast a shadow over her, stifling her jollity. *I'm going to miss him.*

Trust exercises? You blithering idiot!

Callum tried focusing on reprimanding himself instead of the memory of Wynne's soft, luscious body in his arms. He'd shifted to hide what he was feeling, but he suspected his unceremonious exit had the opposite effect. What was it about the woman that turned him into a pea-brained fool?

He paced a half-moon around the camp, close enough to hear Wynne moving about and getting dressed, but far enough away that he couldn't see what she was doing.

The image of her wide, hazel eyes staring up at him in shock and amusement was seared into his retinas. He could practically count the long, dark lashes framing those beautiful eyes. His mind wanted to wander lower, to the other things he'd glimpsed, but Callum shut down that train of thought.

That road leads to madness, old boy, he thought. *Get her to Wickersburg. Make her safe.* Then *you can think about courting the woman.*

Courting? Where had that thought come from? He hardly knew her. Then again, he supposed that was the point of courting, wasn't it? To see if you and the other person would suit?

You're thinking with the wrong head. Bleddyn's dire warning echoed in his mind.

Callum snorted. What did the wolf know?

Wynne's voice drowned out the phantom of his friend's dubious advice. "Alright, Callum. You can come back. I'm decent."

He shifted as he strode back into camp. He was surprised to find that Wynne had finished packing their gear. Callum swung both their packs onto his back, one over each shoulder, before holding out a hand to her.

"Let's give you a chance to stretch your legs, yeah?"

In which a mistake is made

The second day was harder than the first. The stiffness in Wynne's legs worked itself out, but she tired easily. The toll the siphoning sickness had taken on her body made Callum's gut burn with guilt. Fortunately, by the third day, Wynne seemed to be having an easier time of things. It was a good thing too, because the dense forest was thinning.

The two of them were walking hand in hand when they stepped out onto a wide dirt road. Holding hands had slowly shifted from something awkward and shy into something that felt almost... natural. As they walked, Callum managed to think of a few more stories to tell her of his brothers' antics, and she'd shared a few about the people she'd met in her travels. But she never spoke of her childhood or her parents again. And, although he was curious, Callum didn't push.

"Where are we?" Wynne asked.

"The road outside of Wickersburg. It's a big trade route. We should be able to hitch a ride to just about anywhere you'd want to go."

"We?" she echoed.

Callum squeezed her hand again. "You said these men wouldn't give up so easily. I'm not going to just put you on a cart, pat your head, and hope for the best. I promised you I'd see you to somewhere safe, and that's what I'm going to do."

"What about your brothers? Won't they be worried?"

"I'll send a note back to the village, letting them know I've decided to travel for a while. Alasdair will be annoyed but he'll understand."

Wickersburg wasn't a large city, but it was a sizable town, especially when compared to the tiny Snoaksly-on-Barnham. Brick and timber shops lined the broad avenues of Main Street and High Street. There was even a proper restaurant next door to an inn. The sign on the inn's window said "Vacancy" in a pretty, gilt script. A bell chimed as Callum opened the door and gestured Wynne inside.

It was a far cry from the seedy little village tavern, where you could pay a copper to sleep on the barroom floor, or eight coppers for one of the two private rooms. The lobby was comfortably appointed with reading chairs in practical fabrics of good quality in front of large, glazed windows. A thick, woven rug softened their footfalls as they approached the desk.

"How can I help you?" The desk clerk was a young man with thick spectacles and an open, friendly smile.

Perhaps a little too friendly, Callum thought, noting the way the boy's eyes lingered over

Wynne.

"My wife and I need a room. We plan to stay at least one night, perhaps two. We don't need anything fancy, just a bed big enough for two. Oh, and a bath."

The clerk consulted the ledger for a moment. "Cheapest room I have that'll suit is four pence per night. If you're not sure about tomorrow night, I'll have to charge you a holding fee. It's half the room cost. The bath will be another pence."

"That's more than fair." Callum wasn't about to quibble over it. He would've paid full price for both nights if that's what it took to get Wynne somewhere private, away from anyone who might recognize her.

He dug the coins out of his pack and handed them over.

The clerk found a key and placed it on the desk before turning the ledger around and pushing it towards Callum. "Sign here please."

Callum wrote *Mr. & Mrs. Callum Bertram.* He didn't write often, and his handwriting was sloppy to the point of being hardly legible. He suspected that might work in their favor if anyone checked into them later. Perhaps it was foolish to use his actual name, but he ought to still be an unknown quantity in this whole affair.

"Welcome to the Bird and Blue Inn. I hope you enjoy your stay."

"What have you got for me, Tavish?" Clint

barely spared a glance for the boy. His eyes —and hands—were currently full of something much more interesting than the bespectacled hotel clerk.

Ailsa—she was his new favorite—giggled at the boy and blew him a kiss from her place on Clint's lap. Tavish flushed, averting his eyes from Ailsa's bared breasts.

Clint chuckled. "You know you want to look, boy. Might as well enjoy the view while you tell me why the fuck you're bothering me right now."

The whore giggled and Tavish turned an even deeper shade of red. His eyes didn't leave his shoes, though. "I think I saw the girl, sir. The one you told me to be looking for."

Clint's good humor vanished. He shoved the half-naked woman off his lap. She squawked and stumbled into Tavish, who leapt back as if burned.

"Get out of here. This is business," Clint snapped.

Ailsa huffed and grabbed her robe but didn't bother to put it on, walking out of the room with her nose in the air. Clint waited until she'd shut the door behind her.

"Where is she?" he demanded.

"At the inn. She arrived a few hours ago. I would have come sooner, but I had to wait for Peigi—"

"I don't care about that. You will get me the key to her room."

Tavish paled. "I... I don't think I can do that, sir. I'll get fired, sir."

Clint leaned forward in his seat. "You do

this for me, Tavish, and you'll be set for life. You won't need a job clerking at the inn. If you don't do this for me, well... we might have to rethink our arrangement regarding your debts."

"They're my father's debts," Tavish muttered.

"And now they're your debts. Selfish of him to jump in that freezing river, really—but here we are."

The boy's fists balled up, but he had the good sense to keep his damn mouth shut. They both knew Tavish's father hadn't committed suicide, but challenging the official story would be very bad for Tavish's own health and well-being.

"I'll get you the key," he ground out. "But there's something else you should know."

Clint relaxed in his seat, once again lounging comfortably. "And what's that?"

"She isn't alone. She came in with a man. Burly guy. Red hair. Good looking. Seemed like the woodsy sort. They were both covered in dirt, at any rate. He said she was his wife when he asked for the room."

"Are you sure it's her?"

Tavish scowled. "You told me to look for a beautiful blonde girl with hazel eyes that looks like she just spent the last week hiking through the forest. Her dress was even yellow, just like you said."

"She must have picked up a protector somewhere," Clint mused, more to himself than to Tavish. "Did you catch his name?"

"Bertram, I think. Collins Bertram, maybe? Something with a C. It was hard to read."

"Bertram." He rolled the name around in

his head, trying to remember where he'd heard it before. "Forget the key. We need to do this quiet-like, so we're going to have to separate the girl from her bodyguard."

"What are you going to do?"

Clint smiled his gap-tooth smile. "It's not what *I'm* going to do, my boy. It's what *you're* going to do."

In which Goldilocks is Bold

Wynne luxuriated in the steaming water of the bath. It wasn't very big—her knees were practically in her face—but the hot water soothed the aches in her hips and lower back. Riding on a bear's back was hell on the body. The maids had brought good quality soap that smelled of lavender and thick towels for drying off.

She'd been surprised when Callum had requested the bath, but supposed she really shouldn't have been; the man had shown nothing but care for her comfort right from the moment she'd met him.

Callum had ensured the tub was delivered and her clothes taken away for laundering before announcing that he was going out. She would have the room to herself to enjoy her bath in private. In a way, Wynne almost wished he hadn't left; this was entirely too much time alone to think.

Something had changed in days following Wayne's confession. The question was *which* confession? The whole sordid truth about what she was and what she'd done? Or the fact that she desperately wanted to have sex with him? Did it matter? Callum had been kind to her from the start, but in the last few days a tenderness had developed that startled and confused her. And, of course, underneath that tenderness was a heat that took her breath away whenever she caught a glimpse of it in his beautiful eyes.

When I make love to you for the first time, it's going to be in a bed, with all the oil lamps burning.

Well, they had a bed now. And an oil lamp burned merrily on the little table by that bed. Would tonight be the night? A heat that had nothing to do with the water temperature suffused her at the thought.

Wynne leaned back as much as she could. She put her feet out of the tub so that her knees hung over the edge and her upper back rested against its side. Water sloshed onto the floor and dripped off her heels, but Wynne didn't care. The position wasn't exactly comfortable, but it allowed her to slip a hand down to that certain sensitive spot. She remembered the feeling of Callum hard against her, and her breath hitched. A small moan escaped her lips as she imagined it was his hands roaming, stroking.

A knock at the door made her jump.

"Wynne?" Callum's voice called from the other side of the door. "Can I come in?"

She knew he was asking if she was done bathing. In a way, Wynne supposed she was. Sitting up and drawing her feet back in the tub, she answered, "Come in."

Callum slipped into the room, a sack in one hand. "I got you some clothes—" He stopped talking when he caught sight of her.

She'd risen from the water and now stood nude, the bathwater glistening on her skin in the lamplight.

"Wynne..."

Wordlessly, she stepped out of the tub and advanced on him.

"What—"

She pressed a finger to his lips, silencing whatever question he had.

"I believe we have a bed tonight." There was a husky quality to her voice even she didn't recognize.

"We do." His answer was low, dangerous. A knowing gleam had replaced his initial surprise in his eyes.

"And the lamp is lit."

"It is."

Callum's gaze flicked down to her feet and rose slowly, burning over every inch of exposed skin. When his eyes finally me hers again, Wynne leaned towards him, face upturned and eyebrows raised. "Then I believe we have a problem."

Callum didn't need any more of an invitation than that. He dropped the bag and brought both hands up to cradle her face, bringing their lips together gently, but firmly. Wynne's moan of desire matched his, and she melted against him, her arms going around his waist. Bathwater soaked into his shirt, but it didn't matter. Nothing in the world mattered but the feel of his hot lips on hers and the press of their bodies.

"Why are you still dressed?" she teased.

He took off the shirt and tossed it. Immediately her hands were roving over his chest, running through the auburn curls and up over his shoulders till they linked behind his neck. She pulled him in for another searing kiss.

"Damn it, Wynne," he growled. "You're making it hard to be a gentleman."

"Then don't be."

Callum scooped her up in his arms and Wynne's legs wrapped around his waist. Four strides brought them to the bed where he dropped her. Her hands went to the laces of his trousers, shoving them and his underthings down as soon as the knots gave way. He climbed onto the bed, and she retreated, enticing him to follow. When she laid back on the thin pillows, he covered her body with his, kissing her slowly.

Impatient, Wynne nipped his lower lip and sucked it between hers. He growled, a purely feral sound, and pulled back. His honey eyes had darkened with desire, and Wynne felt a thrill knowing she was the cause. Then he *really* kissed her. Fiercely. Deeply. There was no room for thought, no room for breath and Wynne was left gasping for the want of him. One warm, broad hand skimmed up her side. Then he hesitated, his hand burning against her ribs below her breast. Wynne smirked and grabbed his wrist, repositioning his hand where she knew they both wanted it. His thumb brushed over her nipple and a shiver of pleasure shot straight through her. Stars above, it had been so long since a man simply touched her.

"Make love to me, Callum," she whispered. "You promised." *Make love to me,* she thought, *even if it's only pretend.*

He chuckled. "I don't believe I actually promised, Goldie." He let their noses touch as he spoke, and she saw all sorts of promises in his eyes. "But I'm happy to oblige."

Callum's kisses trailed away from her lips, following her jawline to that sensitive spot just below her ear. Wynne moaned as his lips and tongue wandered down the column of her throat to her collarbone. Tangling her fingers in his hair, she tried to guide his head lower.

"Patience," he told her before kissing his way down her sternum, between her breasts. His beard had grown in during their travels and now added a delightful abrasion to his attentions.

He lingered there awhile, teasing her breasts until she was gasping. By the time his meandering journey reached her hip, Wynne thought she might combust.

Wynne made a sharp sound of protest when Callum sat back. She wanted to reach for him, but the intensity of his gaze pinned her in place. Slowly, he lifted her foot, placing a kiss just above her anklebone. He worked his way up her leg, teasing the tender skin of her inner thigh with the scruff of his beard.

"Callum." His name fell from her lips in a strangled plea.

"Yes, sweetheart?" he said, nuzzling her other thigh.

"You're driving me crazy."

He flashed her a wicked grin. "That's the idea." His fingers brushed across the golden curls at her center. "May I?"

"For fuck's sake, Callum. *Yes.*"

The next kiss was shockingly intimate, and a small shout tore itself from Wynne's throat. She bit her hand to quiet herself. Callum seemed to take that as a challenge because something in his ministrations changed and Wynne gave up trying to muffle the sounds they elicited.

She was hovering at the edge, ready to fly into a million pieces, when Callum sat up and repositioned himself.

"Last chance, Goldie." His erection rubbed against her core as he hovered over her. He brushed her hair back from her sweaty brow. "Are you sure?"

Instead of answering him, Wynne wrapped her leg around him, urging him forward with the heel of her foot. Callum might have been made of stone for all she managed to move him.

"I want to hear you say it," he said. His smoldering eyes seemed more golden than brown as they studied her face.

"I want you, Callum," she said. "Right. Now."

He sank into her, and they both groaned. Callum squeezed his eyes shut, his expression somewhere between ecstasy and pain, but he didn't move. Wynne wrapped her arm behind his neck and pulled him closer.

"Move," she whispered, giving his earlobe a nip.

Callum made a sound, half groan and half growl, but rolled his hips. "You really like testing my self-control, don't you?"

"Stars, yes."

The pace he set was languid, the strokes long and deep. Reaching between them, he gently rebuilt the momentum she'd lost.

Wynne's climax slammed into her, and she clung to him, her fingers digging into the taut muscles of his shoulders. His lips devoured her throat and her fingers slipped, nails raking down his back. Callum growled, his restraint snapping.

The loss of him from inside her was sudden and caught Wynne by surprise. Warmth gushed against her thigh as his big body shuddered in her arms. His head sank into the crook between her neck and shoulder, though his weight never fully came to rest on her. They were motionless for several seconds, both panting.

Finally, Callum rolled away and onto his back, pulling the boneless Wynne from the damp spot in the sheets. She settled her head onto his chest. They were both sticky with sweat, but she didn't care.

"Callum?" she asked softly after several minutes.

"Yes, Wynne?"

"We're going to do that again, right?"

She felt his chest shake with silent laughter. "I very much hope so."

Lying in bed next to a sleeping Wynne, Callum stared at the ceiling and wished his curse would allow him to join her in peaceful slumber. The lamp was still burning, and he debated whether he should put it out. He decided it wasn't worth waking Wynne, who was once again sprawled over him, her golden hair tickling his neck. A smile curved her lips and Callum decided it was the expression of a well-sated woman.

He sighed in spite of himself. It was going to be another long, mostly sleepless night.

"Callum?"

"Hmm? I'm sorry, sweetheart. Did I wake you?" he asked softly.

"Not exactly. I wasn't deep asleep."

That elicited a soft laugh from him. "You were snoring."

"I do *not* snore."

Callum rolled them over so he was pinning her gently to the bed.

"Yes, you do," he pronounced, kissing her nose. "And you drool, too." He then proceeded to plant quick little kisses over her cheeks and across the bridge of her nose.

"What are you doing?" Wynne demanded through giggles.

"Kissing your freckles. I've wanted to do that since the moment I saw you."

Her nose wrinkled. "You mean when I was snoring and drooling in your bed?"

"Exactly."

She rolled her eyes and pushed him off her

so she could sit up. He noticed that she didn't bother trying to cover anything, and he let his eyes roam over her boldly.

"Callum."

Her voice was serious, and his smile wavered. *Stars above, don't tell me she regrets it already?*

"I've been thinking," she continued slowly. "I can safely siphon your curse away for a day at a time. With your permission, I'd like to siphon it every other day. You'll still have to deal with less than ideal sleep overall, but —" she paused, searching for the right words — "but at least while we're traveling together you'll have some reprieve."

Callum frowned. Besides her careful phrasing—while they were traveling together? —the siphoning sickness frightened him. The illness made her weaker than a lamb for days, and as much as he'd enjoyed those two nights of peaceful sleep, he couldn't put her health at risk over it.

"Wynne, you don't need to risk yourself for my comfort. I wasn't coming along with you because I thought you were some sort of magic sleep aid." Well, he *had* kind of wondered if she'd broken his curse somehow, but that wasn't quite the same thing.

"I know that, but... well... How do I put this? My gift has been nothing but a curse to me. As soon as my mother realized what I could do, she sold me to the highest bidder. They... they made me do horrific things with my gift." A small sob accompanied the words, and Callum wrapped an arm around her, pulling her tight to his side.

Wynne leaned into the comfort before continuing. "I'll never forget the first time they made me use my gift. The way a fae screams when their soul is shattered and sucked out of their body—that sound is permanently embedded in my brain."

"Wynne, you don't—"

"Yes, I do. I want you to understand. That first time... I stopped when he screamed. I was only eleven, and terrified. When I wouldn't continue, they beat me senseless. But I was too valuable to kill, so when I still refused, they locked me away in small, dark spaces until I would do anything to get out." She shuddered, then looked up to meet his concerned gaze. Tears rimmed her eyes. "I've only been able to use my gift for good a handful of times in my whole life. Please. Let me do this for you."

He wanted to argue. The potential toll on her was severe, and he never wanted her to go through such a thing again, especially not on his account. But the look in her eyes stilled his tongue. This was as much for herself as it was for him. And, he had to admit, she knew her gift and her limits much better than he did.

"Alright." He said the word softly, brushing a lock of unruly hair from her brow. "If it will make you happy, then I won't argue with you. But you have to promise me you won't let yourself get sick again."

She nodded, and he leaned in to seal the deal with a kiss. Unlike their previous passion-crazed exchanges, this was a slow, deliberate caress of lips. As they kissed, Wynne brought her hands up to frame his face. Callum had the briefest impression of a sucking sensation on his skin, and then it was over, and Wynne pulled away. With her went all the heaviness of his curse. He felt light. Free.

"That's amazing."

She smiled at him. "It is, isn't it?"

"And the curse doesn't bother you?"

"The actual siphoning is a bit unnerving—the witch's magic is potent and dark—but it can't hurt me. It can't hurt anyone until I'm forced to release it back into a proper host."

The phrase 'proper host' struck Callum as odd, but he didn't press her. Something in the way she held herself told him that talking about her gift was still uncomfortable. He supposed when you spent your whole life trying to hide something, it was hard to break the habit. Wynne was slowly baring everything to him; mind, body, and magic. He would let her continue to do so at her own pace.

They talked of nothings for a time. Callum didn't know how many minutes or hours passed. It didn't really matter. Eventually, Wynne fell quiet, and he extinguished the lamp. His eyelids felt heavy, and with no curse to fight it, he gently drifted off to sleep.

In which Baby Bear ventures out

The morning started out with such promise. Wynne awoke to a series of kisses that started at her forehead and worked their way down her temple to her cheekbone, to her jaw, and then that delicious spot on her neck. Lips trailed down between her breasts and then lower, stoking the fire inside her. Callum made love to her with the bright sunshine streaming through the room's tiny window.

And then the blasted man had to go and pick a fight.

"I don't need to release it yet. I'm fine!" Wynne repeated for what felt like the hundredth time.

For forty-five minutes after breakfast was delivered, the two of them had debated when Wynne should release the curse back into Callum. He insisted she should put it back as soon as possible each morning and let him deal with it. Meanwhile, Wynne was of the opinion that a few daylight hours without the weariness of carrying around such malignant magic would do him good.

"I just don't want you to get sick again because of me, Wynne. Please."

His eyes had grown dark and intense, and Wynne realized for the first time that Callum was actually scared. Not of her, as she was accustomed to. No, Callum was scared *for* her. She thought about how the siphoning sickness must have seemed from his perspective and shuddered.

"I promise I won't let myself get sick again," she told him, her expression softening. "I'll give the curse back to you this evening after you've had a chance to rest again."

He didn't look convinced, but in the end, Wynne won the argument because she was ultimately the only one with any real control over the situation. With that settled, she thought the rest of the day would go smoothly. Ha!

"We should plan our next steps," Callum said, pulling his shirt on over his head. "Is there somewhere you think you'll be safe?"

Wynne shrugged, wishing she had an answer. She'd always thought that as long as her trail ran cold, her pursuers would give up. Though, after escaping from her first master, she'd never actually stopped running long enough to test the theory. Now she had made an unknown enemy. Unknown, because as much as she feared Clint and what he would do to her, Wynne knew he wasn't working solely on his own behalf. Men like him never were. No, there was someone pulling the strings, someone who had paid good money to have a siphon imbue Clint with that poor fae girl's gift.

"I'm going to scout out our options then."

The way Callum said *he* was going to go made Wynne bristle. This was her life they were talking about. If anyone should be scouting out her options, it should be her, and she told him so.

He held his hands up defensively. "I'm not going to make any decisions or commit us to anything. I'm just going to go see what's around, who is going where. Nobody's looking for me, so I should be able to move around town without alerting anyone to your presence. If you go out there and inquire about travel options, it will be noticed. Men have a way of remembering beautiful young women."

She knew he was right but that didn't mean she had to like it.

Callum must have been able to see it in her expression because he grasped her upper arms gently, his thumbs rubbing in soothing motions through the fabric of her clean chemise. "Look, I know you barely know me, but please trust me on this. I promise where we go will be your decision and I won't hide any of the options from you, no matter how risky I believe them to be. Let me be the one to take some risks, alright? Just like you're doing for me."

"I don't understand you," Wynne admitted. "I don't understand why you would do all this for me."

His smile was so gentle it made her heart squeeze. "I won't pretend that I know entirely myself. There's something about you, Wynne." One hand left her arm to brush a lock of stray hair from her forehead as he spoke. "You make me feel things I've never felt before. They're confusing, and maybe a bit rash, but I don't want to give them up yet. I'd like to see where this adventure takes us."

"Fine, you win. I'll stay here," she said tartly, trying to cover her reeling emotions. What was she supposed to do with an admission like that? His words echoed her own confused feelings. Yes, there was a delicious heat between them. Perhaps it was clouding her judgment, but Wynne was sure she would be an idiot if she claimed that was all there was.

"Why do I feel like I should savor this small victory?" Callum asked. A half smile turned up the corner of those tempting lips.

It annoyed Wynne that those lips were even more tempting now that she knew exactly what they tasted like. She gave in to the temptation, and when they broke apart, that half smile transformed into a full grin.

"Because victory will be rare," she answered.

She laughed when he raised his eyebrows at her and said, "So I've noticed."

It seemed to Callum that the best place to start was actually just down the stairs and down the hallway. The same clerk as before sat at the desk in the lobby. He was slouched in his seat, reading a ragged-looking book with his spectacles perched halfway down his nose. He didn't seem to notice Callum.

"Excuse me."

"Oh!" The young man jerked upright, stuffing the book quickly out of sight in a drawer. "Sorry about that. Checking out?"

"Not quite yet. I was wondering if you could point me in the right direction. My wife and I are looking for transportation. Nothing fancy. We were hoping we might be able to barter for a ride with some outgoing merchants. I understand Wickersburg has a fine export of baskets."

The clerk gave a weak chuckle and scrubbed his mousy hair with one hand. "You might try down by the warehouses."

"The warehouses?" Callum repeated.

"Take a right out of here and follow High Street through to Traders' Row. There's a few shops, but it's mostly warehouses. Any one of them should have caravans outgoing, but you might try Carlisle's first."

"Why Carlisle's?"

The clerk shrugged. "More merchants rent space from Carlisle than anyone else. Just figured you might have a better chance of hitching a ride with more caravans to choose from."

Callum thanked the kid and asked that lunch be sent up for Wynne—sliding some coin across the desk as he did so—before heading for the door. To his chagrin, the weather had turned drizzly while he and Wynne argued. Callum pulled up his hood and headed in the direction the clerk had indicated. He kept his steps brisk though the temptation to linger and explore was strong. He'd only been to Wickersburg a couple of times, and always with Alasdair around to keep the trip strictly business. According to Al, bears didn't belong wandering around in human settlements.

Traders' Row was busy, but it was a different kind of busy than High Street. Instead of people coming and going from shops and lingering around the restaurant, Traders' Row was full of horses and oxen. Drivers hollered at animals and each other. In front of the warehouses, laborers loaded and unloaded crates and barrels from the myriad of carts. The clerk hadn't been kidding when he said just about any warehouse should have caravans heading out. It was no wonder Wickersburg seemed so prosperous.

Carlisle's was at the eastern end of the row. A large, gilded sign above the huge, barn-like doors proclaimed the name in fancy script. Two rows of carts and wagons were parked on either side of the door and at least a dozen men were going back and forth. It seemed the vehicles on the right were being unloaded, while the ones to the left were preparing for departure.

"Can I help you?" a high, squeaky voice said from the vicinity of his elbow.

Callum whirled and found himself looking at the top of a rather tall hat. The owner of the hat was a short, thin man who looked like a good stiff breeze would blow him away. Thick spectacles magnified his eyes and sat on a slim, pointed nose that twitched as he spoke. A surreptitious sniff told Callum all he needed to know: wererat.

"Depends. Do you work here?" Callum asked.

"Vice President of Operations and warehouse manager, Dexter Points at your service, sir," he said with a tip of his hat.

"Callum Bertram." He extended a hand, which the smaller man shook with a firm grip. "I'm looking for a caravan that's taking on passengers. Something departing in the next day or so."

The wererat raised his bushy dark eyebrows so that they peeked over his specs. "No concern as to the destination?"

Callum did his best to smile. These were the sorts of questions he had hoped wouldn't be asked. His cover story was flimsy sounding at best. "My wife and I have decided to travel for a bit, to see where whim and the world take us before we settled down to the business of babies and family."

"Ah, a pair of adventurous souls. If only my wife were so free-spirited. We have six at home at the moment, and three grown would you believe it?"

Considering how prolifically wererats tended to reproduce compared to other werebeasts, Callum really wasn't surprised. There were still some werecats who liked to hunt wererats for sport, even if they staunchly denied it when the bodies were found.

"I never would've guessed," he said though, keeping the conversation friendly.

"All the schedules are in the office," the wererat—Dexter, Callum reminded himself —said as he started walking towards the warehouse. He gestured for Callum to follow. The building had a normal-sized door far to the left of the large one where men and goods were streaming in and out. A sign above it, painted in gold, read "Office."

Callum didn't know what he expected from the office at a warehouse, but he was pretty sure this wasn't it. The wall to the right was covered in papers. Maps marked with ink and pins to indicate trade routes and stops and who knew what else clung to the wall. Pinned next to those were papers with names and dates that Callum assumed must be caravan schedules. Some of them had notes next to them in red ink that said things like "Late" or "Rerouted".

Across from the wall of schedules was a long counter, where several clerks went about their business. It was also loaded down with papers. These were in neat stacks in baskets marked with tags that said things like "Incoming" and "Outgoing". A door behind the counter had a sign pinned to it that read "Authorized Personnel Only." In front of each clerk was a queue of men who looked like they might be caravan masters, clutching papers of their own. Probably bills of lading. Their presence made the room small and suffocating.

"I need just a moment to take care of something and then we'll see what we can find for you, hm?" Dexter went to the far end of the row of clerks, to a pleasant-looking young woman with thick gold curls that reminded Callum of Wynne. The general din of voices muddled what they were saying a bit, but Callum thought he heard the wererat say, "Tilly, m'dear, could you please let Lord Windholt know that his package has arrived."

That bit of business concluded, Dexter ushered Callum into what appeared to be his office. The warehouse manager gestured to a padded leather chair in front of the desk before circling around to sit behind it. He pulled a sheaf of papers out of a drawer and spread them out across the desk.

They spoke for a while, discussing various destinations and the caravans and routes to each. Dexter seemed to be pushing Callum towards certain cities and it was setting the werebear's teeth on edge. He was getting the distinct impression that he was being herded, and he didn't like it one bit.

There was a knock at the door, and one of the girls from the dispatch counter stuck her head in.

"Mr. Points? I'm sorry to interrupt, but Lord Windholt's man is here for his package."

Points sighed heavily. "Send him in, Tilly." To Callum, he said, "Pardon me, this will only take a moment. Tilly's a sweet child, but a bit dim. Can't trust her not to misplace a thing."

Callum didn't return his affable smile. He could smell the werecats as soon as Tilly opened the door. There were at least three, and he knew they weren't here to pick up a package unless the package was him. A cold knot of fear lodged in his stomach. If this was a trap, then that meant that someone knew Wynne was here. They weren't after him—they just needed to keep him distracted long enough to kidnap Wynne.

"Mr. Points," he said, looking the wererat in the eye, "I'm afraid that your lovely office rug is about to be ruined."

Callum leapt out of his seat, shifting and swiveling mid-air. Unprepared, the three men in the doorway found themselves bowled over by fifteen hundred pounds of pissed off bear. He shifted again, running out of the office and through the now empty dispatch. As he burst through the outer door and out into the rain, pain like fire ripped across his shoulders. One of the cats had shifted and raked his wicked claws down his back. With a bellow, Callum shifted again and ran out into the yard, sending panicked workers scurrying.

The problem was, Callum was never going to win a foot race with a cougar or whatever the other men were. He just didn't have the speed whether on four legs or two. He was going to have to stand and fight, but preferably somewhere that all three of them couldn't swarm him at once.

One of the cats came up alongside him, snarling. It lunged, trying to sink its teeth into his jugular. Callum backhanded it in the face and kept running. Another leapt at him from behind, its vicious claws tearing into the flesh of his back and side, creating rivers of blood under his coat. Callum bellowed but kept running.

People were screaming and running in all directions. Horses squealed and reared. Callum darted between two coaches, sending the horses into a frenzy. Behind him, one of the big cats yelped, and he heard a coachman's screams. He didn't turn to look.

The air gusted from his lungs as he ran. Callum didn't even know where he was going, only that he had to get away before he could help Wynne. He made a sharp right, cutting into an alley between two of the huge brick buildings. A rusty metal ladder that was probably meant for escaping fires clung to the side of one of them. Callum shifted and scurried up the ladder. Adrenaline kept him moving through the burning pain that wrapped around his body. The skin of his back and his clothes were shredded. He was dripping blood everywhere. They were no hounds or bears, but even those damn mountain lions ought to be able to track him.

The window of the second story wasn't open, but Callum didn't have time to feel guilty about breaking it. The glass, cheap and bubbled, shattered easily. Since the window was designed to be a fire escape, Callum fit through it easily. He stumbled through the frame, landing on his knees and palms in the fragments of the broken pane. The blood loss was getting to him.

"Don't move."

Callum looked up to find himself face to face with the business end of a crossbow.

"Please. Help me," he begged.

Whatever the owner of the crossbow

might have said next, Callum didn't know. Adrenaline could no longer mitigate the effects of severe blood loss, and the darkness lingering at the edges of his vision closed in.

In which disaster strikes

After Callum left, Wynne found herself at a loss. With nothing better to do, she flopped down on the bed, staring at the ceiling and daydreaming. She conjured up images of all the naughty things she and Callum could get up to together. When her imaginings wandered into other territory—emotionally dangerous territory— she'd think up some new fantasy to distract herself.

A knock on the door snapped Wynne out of her stupor. She scrambled off the bed and crossed the room to answer it. If it was Callum, he would have just come in after knocking, so she hoped it was lunch. Her stomach rumbled its agreement.

Instead of a maid, Wynne was surprised to find the front desk clerk standing in the hall with a tray of food that smelled absolutely divine. He stammered his way through an explanation. "Your husband overpaid for lunch, so I, uh, thought maybe you'd enjoy something from the restaurant next door."

"Thank you, that's very kind of you," she said, smiling as she took the tray from him. The young man blushed and looked down at his feet.

"It was no problem, ma'am. Enjoy your lunch."

"Thank you, I will."

Wynne shut and locked the door before carrying the tray to the bedside table. Several crusty rolls and a dish of butter accompanied a large bowl of some sort of chowder. The scent of it made her mouth water. She tore one of the rolls in half and scooped out a big bite of the soup. It was so good, creamy and full of sweet corn and little chunks of early carrots. It was a shame Callum was missing out on it.

The bowl was empty too soon, and Wynne flopped back on the bed, sated.

Suddenly, her limbs felt heavy. Too heavy. Too suddenly. She knew this feeling. Alarmed, Wynne tried to sit up, but her body wouldn't respond. Her eyes closed of their own accord. Just before the blackness took her, all she could think was, *Fuck.*

Tavish paced the laundry room anxiously. How long would it take her to eat the soup? How long would it take for the sleeping draught to take effect? The witch in Clint's employ had promised it was "fast acting" but what did that even mean?

Stop stalling, Tavish, he told himself. *Just*

go knock on the door. If she answers, then it hasn't done its job yet. Just tell her you're there for the tray.

He grabbed one of the big cotton bags the maids used for hauling the copious amount of laundry the hotel produced. He balled it up and stuck it under one arm, hoping that would make it less conspicuous; his duties didn't include helping with the wash.

When the woman didn't answer the door, Tavish took a deep breath and fingered through his keyring. The sound of the lock turning seemed unbearably loud.

She was half lying on the bed, like she'd been sitting when the spell took ahold. He noted with a great degree of embarrassment that she was only wearing a thin chemise. Should he try to dress her before taking her to Clint?

In the end, Tavish decided it was best just to hurry up and get her out of there as quickly as possible. The witch hadn't been very specific about how long the effects of her spell would last. He shook out the bag and loosened the drawstring as far as it would go. He'd have to sort of fold the woman up to make her fit in the bag.

In the end, she was sitting in the bottom of it with her knees tucked up to her chest and her head lolling against the side of the bag. Tavish was sweating and huffing when he drew the drawstring closed. She wasn't a large woman, but she was still heavier than he'd expected. He only hoped he'd be able to get her down the stairs without hurting her.

The inn had separate stairs for the

servants. They were narrow and nobody other than the maids—who had mostly finished their morning duties—used it. They should be done changing sheets and delivering meals by now.

"I regret putting you on the third floor," he muttered to the sleeping woman in the bag.

He took the stairs a few at a time. Each time he paused, he let his burden rest against the step on what he hoped was her bum. They'd just made it to the second-floor landing when Tavish heard the sound he'd dreaded; the door on the first floor creaked open. It was followed by footsteps that made the old stairs squeak.

"Tavish!" It was Gillian, one of the kitchen girls. She was carrying a tray full of eggs and bacon. Apparently, one of their guests was late to rise. Her eyes flicked down to the bag at his feet, and he thought his heart might stop. "What are you doing?"

"Oh. Um, Abbie asked me to get the laundry from 302. She forgot it this morning. You know how Abbie is." He was pretty sure Gillian didn't believe him, but it was a plausible story. Abbie was sweet, but forgetful and prone to shirking her duties.

Fortunately, Gillian shrugged as if what he was really up to wasn't worth her time to investigate. "You should talk to Mistress Cordle about her, Tavish." Mistress Cordle was the head housekeeper. "You shouldn't be doing her work for her."

"Oh... yes. Perhaps I should. Thank you, Gillian."

"I'd best get this up to Mr. Woolsworth.

You know how he gets when his breakfast is cold, the old goat." Gillian brushed past him on the narrow landing and Tavish held his breath, praying she wouldn't accidentally kick the bag. He waited until he heard the door on the third floor open and close before continuing down the steps. That was far too close for comfort.

One of Clint's men—a weaselly fellow with a bad case of laryngitis—was waiting at the back door of the inn. Tavish handed the bag over to him with a mixture of relief and regret. He hated being a party to this. He was trying really hard not to think about what Clint might want with a pretty young woman like this one.

"For your trouble," the man rasped, tossing a sizable leather purse to him.

Tavish stuck it into his shirt. Shame burned his cheeks. He didn't even count it. It didn't matter. No amount of coin would erase his guilt.

"Tell Clint I'm out. I'm leaving Wickersburg."

The man shrugged and picked up the laundry bag. The way he swung it over one shoulder like it didn't have a person in it made Tavish wince.

"That's probably for the best," the man said. "You don't want to be here when her friend comes looking for her. Werebears get grouchy about their women."

"Werebears?"

The man tapped his nose. "I can smell 'im on her through the bag. I doubt a couple days of rutting are enough for the beast. Best watch your back, boy." And with that, he started down the alley, carrying his burden as if it were nothing.

"I hope you know what you've gotten yourself into," Arlo said as he dumped a laundry bag on the floor of the brothel's kitchen.

Clint eyed him curiously. The man had been scared and sullen ever since their encounter with the woodsman the day the siphon girl had gone missing. Clint had bribed and threatened till he was blue in the face to get the man to retrieve the girl from the inn. It wasn't until he agreed to spend a small fortune on a scent masking charm that Arlo had finally agreed. But whatever it was that Arlo knew, the tight-lipped bastard wasn't sharing it.

"Open it."

Arlo rolled his eyes but loosened the sack's drawstring and let the top fall to reveal a head of golden hair.

Clint chuckled. "So, the kid held up his end of the deal, did he?" he asked.

Arlo grunted in affirmation.

Clint would never admit it aloud, but he'd been worried about the viability of his own plot. Tavish had always been a reliable informant, but that was a far cry from kidnapping. He'd half expected that Arlo would have to retrieve the girl himself.

Clint heaved the girl up by her armpits while Arlo disentangled the bag from her limbs. Then he scooped her up, one arm under her knees and the other supporting her back. Her head lolled back, and her glorious hair fell in shining waves. Clint let his eyes rove over her body appreciatively, feeling himself harden. He would have paid the boy extra if he'd known the girl was coming in a state of partial undress. His only regret was that she wouldn't be awake to enjoy his attentions.

"The boss doesn't want her harmed," Arlo reminded him in that grating voice of his.

"She'll still be in one piece when I'm done with her," Clint said, moving to the stairs. "So long as she can still use her gift, the boss won't mind."

"I do mind, very much," a smooth voice announced.

Clint jerked around to face the door leading out to the front of the establishment. Lord Windholt strolled into the room, the heels of his riding boots clicking on the stone floor.

He smiled at Arlo. "Thank you for informing me of the girl's whereabouts, Arlo. You're dismissed."

Arlo bowed and ducked out the back door into the alley behind the whorehouse.

"I'm disappointed in you, Clint." The pleasant smile he'd worn for Arlo turned nasty when he fixed his gaze upon him. "You failed to inform me that the girl had been found."

"How did you—"

"I have my means. Distance is no object. I hope you'll remember that in the future, Clint." Windholt snapped his fingers and three more men crowded into the small kitchen. "You"—Windholt pointed to one of the men—"take the girl and put her in the carriage."

Clint knew he didn't have a choice and handed over his prize without complaint, watching with longing as the man carried her out of the kitchen. If he was patient, he'd get another chance at her.

Once the girl was safely out the door, Windholt turned back to Clint with a wide smile that made the thug's blood run cold. He knew that smile, and he didn't like it one bit.

"You two," Windholt said, addressing the other men he'd brought with him. They were big and burly, the sort who were probably werebeasts or otherwise magically enhanced. "See that Clint here remembers who works for whom."

"You got it, boss," the bigger of the two said, grabbing Clint by the front of his shirt. "Let's go, Clint. We're going to have a nice little chat out in the woods."

In which Goldilocks meets her captor and Baby Bear makes a friend

Waking up from magically induced sleep was really something, Wynne decided. If she dreamt, she didn't remember it. The whole experience was more like having a chunk cut out of one's memory than actually sleeping. One moment she was eating a delicious bowl of soup in her hotel room, and the next she was sitting half-dressed in a carriage with a stranger.

"Ah, the sleeping beauty is finally awake." A well-dressed gentleman sat opposite her. A walking cane and top hat rested on the seat beside him. His blond hair was slicked back with pomade, the ends curling at the nape of his neck. He gave her a smooth smile that did not reach his stony gray eyes.

"Where am I, and who are you?"

The gentleman laughed. Unlike Callum's bright guffaws, there was something sinister in this man's chuckles. Something that made

Wynne's skin crawl. "Where are my manners? My name is Ainsley Crichton, Lord of Windholt. And I'm sure you are observant enough to realize that you are in a carriage."

"Where is the carriage, then?" She wasn't in the mood for pedantic word games.

"Why, on a road of course."

"Fine then," she snapped. "Don't tell me where we are. I suppose you won't tell me where we're going, either."

He tsked. "Alas, my beauty, I don't think I can quite trust you with that information yet. But you're being quite rude. I've shared my name; it's only fair that you do the same."

"Goldie." She tried not to wince. As much as she didn't want to give this creep her real name, she hated the idea of Callum's nickname for her on this man's lips.

"Goldie." He repeated it several times, as if tasting it. "Goldie. Hmm, no I don't think it suits you at all, my dear."

Wynne lifted her chin. "Well, it's my name, so you might as well get used to it."

This elicited another chuckle. Something sparked in his eyes that she didn't like at all; the way he looked at her left an oily sensation on her skin. "Oh, you've got some spirit in you," he said. "No wonder Clint was so enamored with you."

"Clint is enamored with anything he thinks he can stick his cock into."

At this, Windholt positively roared with laughter, slapping his knee with his riding gloves. Eventually, he composed himself, although a few stray chuckles still emerged.

Wynne wished he would just shut up and get to the point. "So, are you going to tell me what I'm doing here or what?"

He sobered instantly.

"Oh, I think you know exactly what you're doing here, my little siphon."

Wynne gave him her best scoff. "I don't know what you're talking about."

His eyes took on a dangerous glint as he leaned towards her. "Oh, I think you do, Goldie. You know exactly what I'm talking about. Tell me, how have you gone so long without being harnessed?"

"You've got the wrong girl. I'm just an ordinary woman who happened to run afoul of Clint in a bar. It's been an unfortunate acquaintance for everyone involved."

The back of Windholt's hand connected with her face, and she tasted blood.

He leaned back in his seat, studying her with icy eyes. "There now, see what you made me do? I'm very disappointed in you, Goldie. Lying is not very ladylike. I don't want to hurt you, but I need you to be honest with me."

Wynne tongued the cut on the inside of her stinging cheek. She knew it was the least of what she had to look forward to.

"Let's say for the sake of argument that I am who you think I am. What are you planning to do with me?"

He spread his arms wide and graced her with another broad smile that still didn't reach his eyes. "Why, I'm going to give you everything you've ever wanted. Wealth.

Comfort. A place to belong. All you have to do is use your gift for a few teensy little jobs every now and again."

"Did it ever occur to you that what I want most is to be left alone?"

"Ah, my beauty." He did his best to feign a sad expression. "I'm afraid that's the one thing a creature like you can never have. You're far too dangerous to be left unsupervised."

"If I'm so dangerous, why aren't you nervous about being alone in this carriage with me?"

"Because I don't have any innate magic for you to steal. And know this, my beauty—I don't need any of my hard-won gifts to hurt you."

The carriage rattled to a stop.

"Don't get excited, lovely," Windholt continued. "We're just taking a quick stop. A guard will be right outside to ensure you stay put. In the meantime, please feel free to dress more appropriately. Everything you ought to need is in that bag." He pointed to a sack on the seat next to her that Wynne hadn't noticed before. "I will be back shortly. Do behave." And with that, he alighted from the carriage.

Wynne didn't move until the door slammed shut. Then she dug frantically through the sack. There was a pair of silk hose, delicately embroidered with pink roses; a fine linen chemise edged in lace and silk ribbons; silk petticoats with yet more lace; a set of stays; and the skirt and bodice to a fine silk gown in shades of rose and blush. Dainty pink silk slippers matched the whole ensemble.

She ignored the underthings and chemise. Her own would do, and she wasn't about to strip naked when that Ainsley fellow could come back at any moment. Instead, she pulled on the stockings and petticoats before struggling into the corset. It wasn't made for her. The woman it was tailored for was much longer in the torso and had less of a bust. Wynne's breasts would spill out and it would no doubt dig into her hips when she sat. The gown itself wasn't a bad fit but was a ridiculous outfit for traveling with far too much trimming for Wynne's taste. The shoes were too big, of course. Why bother giving her something she could actually walk in?

The carriage door popped open, and her captor climbed in gracefully.

"Ah, much, much better. You are a vision, my dear," Windholt said with mock gallantry.

Wynne bit back a hot retort. Her expression betrayed her, though, because Windholt started laughing again.

"Don't you look positively murderous! Not to worry, lovely. You'll be able to commission a wardrobe more suited to your tastes in due time. For now, I'm afraid you'll have to make do with what *I* find becoming. And what I have available. It is a pleasing dress, don't you think?"

"Gorgeous," she said through gritted teeth.

"That's the spirit. I think we're going to get on swimmingly, my dear." He rapped on the ceiling of the coach with his cane and the vehicle lurched into motion. His eyes swept up and down her, lingering where her breasts threatened to spill out of the bodice. "Yes, we're going to get along just fine."

"Oh good, you're awake."

"Wynne?" The name escaped Callum's lips like a plea.

"I'm afraid not," an unfamiliar voice replied.

Callum groaned and pushed himself up on his elbows. He was lying on his stomach in an unfamiliar bed. A pleasant looking woman with dark ringlets sat on a stool next to him. The smell of herbs and magic filled the dimly lit room and made his nose itch. Most of the magic smell, he noted, was coming from her. Probably a witch. Definitely some sort of healer.

"We were a little afraid that you weren't going to wake up," she said. "You suffered quite a lot of blood loss."

"Where am I?"

"My cousin's home. He brought you here after you came crashing through his office window."

"The man with the crossbow?" Callum guessed. He couldn't remember the man's face, but he definitely remembered the bolt aimed at his head.

"Reggie decided you weren't much of a threat when you passed out on him. I'm Isabel, by the way, but you can call me Izzy," she said, holding out a hand to him that he shook awkwardly. "You're lucky Papa and I were visiting. Even with your werebeast healing, I'm not sure you would've survived without a little help."

"You're a witch." It wasn't exactly an accusation.

Izzy shrugged. "Something like that. My powers aren't exactly... reliable. I can whip up a blood boosting draught with the best of them though. Lucky thing for you."

"How long have I been here?"

"Since yesterday afternoon. It's just about dawn now."

Callum cursed and tried to sit up. His back and sides screamed with half-knit wounds. Souvenirs from his run-in with the werecats.

"Where the hell do you think you're going!?" the witch screeched. "You're in no condition to be getting out of that bed. You werebeasts heal fast, but not that fast. Some of those cuts are serious!"

"I have to get back to the inn. I'm not their target. This was—" He panted with pain as he forced his body to sit up. "A distraction. My..." He hesitated. How did he explain Wynne to a stranger? "They're after my friend, and she can't defend herself. I have to get back to her."

"A friend, huh? You called her name an awful lot for just a friend."

If she was trying to embarrass him, it wasn't going to work. "Give me another blood draught and do whatever else you can to close up these wounds."

Her dark eyebrows arched. "Oh really? Demanding, aren't you?"

Callum closed his eyes and prayed for

patience.

"I'm sorry. Izzy, was it? I'm very grateful for your help and I will gladly reimburse you and your cousin for the trouble and property damage. However, it is imperative that I get back to the Bird and Blue as quickly as possible."

Somewhere deep inside, he knew it was too late. If they'd known where to find him, then they knew where to find Wynne. Still, the inn was the last place she'd been, and the trail would start there. He should be able to track her.

Stars, I'm so sorry Wynne, he thought. *I was so foolish.*

Callum was fighting tears when Izzy sighed. "I'll see what I can do. Like I said, my magic isn't the most reliable thing, but I can mix up potions with generally positive results."

It was all Callum could do to contain himself over the next several hours as the witch mixed and ground, poured and stirred. Her setup, he noticed, was a rather unconventional. Instead of an iron cauldron or even a cooking pot, Izzy went about her potion-making with glass vials and beakers. Instead of using a stove or hearth, she heated her mixtures carefully over something similar to an oil lamp. About the only thing he recognized as traditional witches' gear was a mortar and pestle that appeared to be made of quartz.

Eventually Izzy set one of the concoctions aside to cool while the other simmered on the strange little heating apparatus.

"Let's get those bandages off then," she announced.

Rather than moving him to untie them, she snipped through the fabric with a small pair of scissors. Then she tested the temperature of her cooling mixture on the inside of her wrist. Apparently satisfied, she began working it into the wounds on his back. Callum hissed at the pain.

"So, tell me about this Wynne," Izzy said as she worked. "What's she like?"

"Brave. Kind—Ouch, that hurts."

"You'll live. So brave and kind, huh? Pretty, too, I suppose?"

"Beautiful," Callum replied without thinking. Izzy prodded a cut a little harder than he thought was strictly necessary, so he added, "Inside and out. She's always taking me by surprise."

"Sounds like you love her."

"I've only known her a week." He sighed. This woman was never going to meet Wynne or his brothers. How much of a fool he was would never get back to anyone if he told her the truth. His voice broke a little as he spoke, "But I think I could love her. I want to find out, but I can't do that if she's been kidnapped and imprisoned stars know where."

"Hey," Izzy said softly, leaning sideways to look him in the eye. "Look at me. I promise you I'm doing everything I can to get you back on your feet as quick as I can, okay?"

"Thank you, Izzy."

"I think the blood booster should be about done. You just rest and let the salve do its job while I finish that up. We'll have you back to the Bird and Blue before you know it."

In which Baby Bear goes hunting

Wynne was gone.

The Bird and Blue Inn didn't look any different, but Callum knew even before he got to their room that it was true. There was no evidence of a struggle. It looked like she'd just walked out—without half her clothes. Her yellow kirtle had been cleaned and set on the dresser. The pretty blue one he'd bought her was still in the sack by the door where he'd dropped it the night they'd made love. Not a single thing was out of place.

Except the smell.

When he'd left that afternoon, the room had smelled of Wynne and bear and sex. Now there were other scents jumbled in the mix. One was a human male that smelled vaguely familiar and the other filled him with dread. Magic.Callum's back thumped against the wall as his knees went weak. He grunted at how that irritated his wounds, but he couldn't find it in himself to remain standing and sunk to the floor. Tears welled in his eyes, and he had to scrub them away with the heel of his palm.

"You never should have left her alone, you star burned idiot." Even as he said the words aloud, he knew the opposite wouldn't have been much better. He shuddered to think what that business with the werecats would have been like if Wynne had been with him.

A knock on the doorframe drew his attention.

"Mr. Bertram?" A young woman—one of the maids, judging by her uniform—stood in the doorway of the room. "Do you have a moment?"

"What can I do for you?"

She studied him with serious dark eyes. "It's what I may be able to do for you, Mr. Bertram. Your wife is missing, isn't she?"

Callum scrambled to his feet. "Do you know something?"

"Tavish—the front desk clerk—also went missing sometime yesterday afternoon."

"And you think he has something to do with Wy—with my wife's disappearance?"

The girl bit her lip. For a moment she looked uncertain, but then something like resolution hardened her expression. "Before he went missing, Tavish was behaving oddly. I ran into him in the servants' stairwell. He was lugging around what looked like a very heavy bag of laundry. It was odd because Tavish never helps with the laundry. He said Abbie had forgotten to collect from one of the rooms and he was doing her a favor. The thing is, when I spoke to Abbie later, she had no idea what I was talking about."

"And you think—"

"That your wife was in the bag, yes. Later, one of the guests asked about having dinner brought up from the restaurant next door. He said he'd overheard Tavish telling your wife that you'd overpaid for her lunch, so he'd brought her something nice from next door. We don't do that; it's against company policy."

A horrible picture was starting to take shape in Callum's mind. Wynne, with no reason to suspect the hotel clerk, would have eaten whatever he brought her. After all, they'd already had several meals from the hotel. That meal was surely laced with something, and that was the magical residue he was smelling in the room. Then the bastard had come back and stuffed Wynne in a laundry bag to haul her out the back.

"I'm going to need any information you can give me on this Tavish fellow." Callum didn't recognize the dark timbre of his own voice.

"You should go to the town watch," the girl said, wringing her hands.

"There's no time for that!" His shout surprised him, and he had to take a deep breath to calm himself. "I'm sorry. Please, I know this isn't your fault. I don't have time to waste on the watch and their questions. Besides, they're probably in the pockets of the men who stole her, anyway."

"I don't know Tavish well, and I doubt the bosses will want to give out his private information. What I can tell you is that he lives on Walkins Ave on the east side of town. He mentioned it once in passing. I don't know the house number though, I'm sorry."

They didn't even have house numbers in Snoaksly-on-Barnham. The idea of there being enough houses to require numbering them made Callum's head swim a bit. It didn't matter, though. She'd pointed him in the right direction; his nose could do the rest.

"Thank you, Miss...?"

"Gillian." She turned to leave, but then paused. Those intense dark eyes studied him for a long moment. "I hope you find her, Mr. Bertram."

"Thank you, Gillian."

When the maid was gone, Callum shut the door and set about sniffing every square inch of the room. He didn't care if it made him look like a damn bloodhound. He was going to memorize every nuance of that bastard's scent, and he was going to find Wynne. Eventually, he felt he'd separated out which odor belonged to Tavish, and he made his way out of the room and down the hall. The trail led down the servants' stairs, as Gillian had said. A whisper of the scent of Wynne and clean cotton lingered there as well. Callum followed it down the stairs and out the back door of the inn.

In the alley behind the inn, Wynn's scent just... stopped. Tavish, meanwhile, was still clearly scented, heading out of the alley onto High Street. Callum suspected that magic was being used to hide Wynne's scent and that she wasn't with Tavish anymore. Likely, he had handed her off to one of Clint's goons before taking off.

Callum stalked out of the alley, following Tavish's trail. He huffed in frustration, wishing he could shift; tracking was much easier on four-legs than two. The sight of a giant bear wandering around their streets for the second time in as many days would probably be too much for the people of Wickersburg though. He'd have the town watch on him in no time. Humans were fully aware that werebeasts existed, but it was considered bad form to flaunt that fact in the middle of predominately human settlements.

He wasn't surprised when the trail led him to Walkins Ave, just as Gillian had said. It was a narrow little street on the outskirts of town. The houses here were shabby, but seemingly as well-kept as their residents could afford. Tavish's home was at the far end of the street, next to a burned-out lot that looked like it might once have been a church.

A middle-aged woman was sweeping the front stoop where Tavish's trail ended. "Can I help you?" she asked when she noticed Callum lingering at the gate.

"I'm looking for Tavish."

The woman stopped sweeping. She suddenly looked much older and very tired. "Mr. Bertram, I assume?"

"That's correct."

"Tavish said you'd probably be stopping by." She sighed. "The boy's gone. And before you ask, I don't know where. He just threw some things in a bag and said that a Mr.

Bertram would undoubtedly be stopping by. He said to tell you that he doesn't have her and that a man named Arlo took her to Clint."

The name Arlo didn't mean anything to him, but at the sound of Clint's name, his blood ran cold. He'd already suspected that's who had taken Wynne, but having it confirmed was something else entirely.

His expression must have been thunderous because the woman suddenly looked close to tears.

"Tavish is a good boy. Whatever he's done, it's not his fault. Those men made him do it." She shuddered. "He just didn't want to end up in the river like his father."

Callum supposed he shouldn't be surprised. It didn't make sense that such a bumbling young man would be deeply involved in a vicious crime syndicate or whatever it was Wynne had stumbled into.

"Please don't hurt him," the woman continued. "Please. He's just a boy."

"I have no intention of hurting your son, ma'am." *Much.*

It was cold in the abandoned warehouse. Well, perhaps abandoned was the wrong word. Between legal occupants was more accurate. Someone would buy it up soon enough and kick out the vagabonds that had taken up residence. Tavish would be gone long before that happened.

He punched the balled-up mass of his cloak, trying to beat it into a more comfortable pillow. It didn't really work, and Tavish flopped down on his back with a sigh, staring up at the timbered ceiling. Sunlight was streaming through the warehouse's dirty glazed windows. It was late morning. Somehow, he'd managed to sleep late, despite the discomfort. It was probably past time he headed for Carlisle's and jumped on the first cart out of town.

Gathering up his things didn't take long. Tavish had packed little more than a change of clothes and a blanket. He'd kept enough of the money from the job to keep his belly full once he was on the road and left the rest for his mother.

A commotion at the front of the warehouse stopped him cold. He knew that voice.

"—a young man, about this tall. He may be wearing spectacles."

Stars save me, he thought. *The bear found me.*

He couldn't let himself be caught. If they found his mauled body in some back alleyway, what would his mother say? He couldn't put her through another death like that. It was bad enough that he was leaving her, even if the coin Clint had paid him would keep her comfortable for years to come.

The other squatters were ratting him out. He couldn't make out what they were saying, but he could imagine them pointing towards the back of the warehouse where Tavish huddled behind some old crates. No honor amongst thieves, it would seem.

"Tavish?" the werebear's voice rose in volume. "Tavish, I know you're back there. Your mother wants you home in one piece, so I suggest you don't make this more difficult than it needs to be."

Tavish shot to his feet in spite of himself. "You better not have hurt my mother!"

Callum Bertram rounded the crates and folded his arms, staring down at Tavish, who suddenly felt very small and spindly.

"You must have me confused with the bastards you work for," the big man said. "Your mother is fine, apart from being worried sick about her bellend of a son."

Shame flooded Tavish, and he looked down at his feet. The last thing he wanted to do was hurt his mother. Stars knew she'd had enough pain in her life. It must have terrified her when this brute showed up demanding her son show himself.

A heavy sigh startled him into looking up at his pursuer.

"You don't strike me as a hardened criminal, and from what your mother tells me you didn't have a whole lot of choices in the matter. So, why don't you make things right as best you can and tell me who took my wife from you?"

"It was a guy named Arlo that picked her up, but he's just an errand boy like me. Clint's the one who wanted her."

A yelp escaped Tavish when he was lifted bodily by the front of his shirt. The big man wrenched him upwards till their noses were almost touching.

"Where. Is. He."

"H-he l-likes to hang out at t-the brothel," he stuttered.

"Where?" Callum demanded. Tavish could have sworn his eyes were glowing.

"C-Colman St-Street."

The front of his shirt was released, and Tavish slumped to the ground.

"Go home. Your mother is worried."

Tavish looked up, surprised to see the big man was already walking away. "You're... you're not going to hurt me?"

The werebear looked back over his shoulder at him. "I don't hurt children. Besides, you're just a pawn. I have bigger game to hunt."

In which an uneasy truce begins

The brothel was quiet in the early afternoon, but Callum had no trouble recognizing it. He could smell it long before he could see it; the stink of human sweat and sex carried on the breeze and made his nostrils itch. It was such a cacophony of competing odors that it was hard to say if Clint's was among them. It was an aging two-story building that was doing its best to look fresh. Rose bushes lined either side of the porch and someone had given it a fresh coat of paint—but the front steps creaked under his boots.

"Can I help you?" a voice asked from his left.

Callum glanced at the woman sprawled out on a wicker chaise, a pipe dangling from her lips. She had the air of a woman trying desperately to cling to the beauty of her younger years. Her cheeks were rouged to imitate the fresh glow of youth, and her hair curled into ebony ringlets, but the lines around her eyes and the pipestem clenched in her teeth marred thc illusiuii.

"I'm looking for someone. Rumor has it he spends a lot of time here."

"Well, now." She paused to blow a smoke ring in his direction. "That would be a breach of customer privacy."

"His name is Clint. Big, bald man with tattoos and bad teeth."

There was a flash of recognition in the woman's dark eyes, Callum was sure of it, but she recovered quickly, taking another long pull from the pipe. "If you want to get your dick wet, you've come to the right place. Otherwise, I'm going to have to ask you to buzz off." She eyed him up and down. "I don't think you'd have trouble convincing one of the girls to give you a go."

"I'm not interested in any of your ladies."

"One of the boys then?"

Callum bit back a growl of frustration. "I need to find Clint. He took something."

"If you've got that kind of business with him, you should know that we don't welcome those sorts of exchanges here. They tend to get messy in all the wrong ways."

"My friend. He took my *friend*."

A flicker of unease crossed the woman's features. It was gone in an instant, hidden behind a mask of boredom, but there was no mistaking it; she knew something.

"I think you should leave."

"Please, if you know something—"

"I know the men you are dealing with are not to be crossed," she snapped, sitting up straight on the chaise.

"They took her and they're going to do

stars know what to her. Do you really want to protect monsters who abduct young women for their own gain?"

She tilted her head, eyeing him speculatively. "Boy, you sure don't know much about the sex trade in this kingdom, do you? You think all those girls in there are here by choice?" She pronounced girls like *gehls* and Callum wondered where she'd been taken from.

"Then why the *fuck* would you wish that on someone else if you could do something to prevent it?" It was a struggle to keep his volume low, his tone civil.

The woman continued to study him, drawing several more puffs on the pipe. At last, she removed it and blew a cloud of smoke at him. The smell was overwhelming, and Callum had to resist the urge to sneeze.

"Hypothetically speaking," she said, gesturing with the pipe. "If I were to tell you that the man you're looking for is upstairs sleeping off a beating and a hangover, what exactly would you do about it?"

"For now, I'd just want to talk."

"And if he doesn't want to talk with you?"

"Then we'll just have to take it outside."

She leaned back on the chaise and took another puff. "You're a fool to involve yourself in this. I hope she's worth the heap o' trouble you're bringing down on your head."

"I'm already involved, and I've already had my share of the trouble." He lifted the hem of his shirt to reveal the still-healing claw marks wrapping around his abdomen.

"Ah, so you're the bear the Hardy triplets were after. Bad move making an enemy out of that lot."

"They started it."

"Liam—the stupid one—he took a pair of horse's hooves to the head on your account. Those boys won't be forgetting you any time soon. I suggest you get out of Wickersburg; his brothers are going to be out for your blood, Bear."

"I'm not leaving without seeing Clint."

"Your funeral. Up the stairs, right-hand hallway. It'll be the second door on your left. Just make sure Ailsa doesn't get caught up in your bullshit."

The front room—Callum supposed you could call it a parlor—was mostly empty. A lone guest sat at a table drinking a cup of tea and reading a newspaper. The other various tables and settees were vacant. A wide staircase dominated the far side of the room, with doors to either side of it. Whomever had designed the staircase had attempted to make it appear grand, with carved railings and red carpet that ran up the middle. But the carpet was worn threadbare, and the carvings were shoddy, clumsy things. Perhaps in the poor light of the evening and the haze of alcohol, it would seem more impressive.

The landing at the top of the stairs was dim. Light from downstairs and the windows at the ends of the two parallel hallways provided the only illumination. Callum followed the woman's directions and knocked on the second door on the left of the right wing. When there was no answer, he knocked harder, making the door rattle on its hinges.

A pretty redhead opened the door just a crack. "Sorry, but I'm already with a client. I think Eileen is free."

Callum put a hand on the door to block her from shutting it. "I'm not here for your services. I'm here to speak with Clint."

There was a flash of fear in her eyes and Callum studied what little of her he could see more closely. Bruises were forming at her throat.

"He's sleeping right now. Perhaps you should come back later—" She tried to push the door closed, but she was no match for a burly werebear. Unable to shut the door on him, Ailsa gave up and stepped back. The door banged off the wall as Callum charged in. A body in the bed jerked awake, and it took Callum a second to recognize the man squinting at him through two ugly black eyes.

"Aw, fuck," Clint muttered before falling back against the pillows.

Callum turned his attention back to the girl, who couldn't have seen more than twenty summers. His eyes skimmed away from her state of undress. "Could you give us a few moments, miss?" His gaze moved to Clint's prone form and the muscles of his face tightened. "I'm afraid this could get ugly."

Ailsa didn't need to be asked twice. She grabbed a dressing gown and scurried out before it was even belted about her waist. Callum shut the door behind her.

"I suppose you're here about the siphon girl," Clint said, pushing himself back up into a sitting position. "I'm surprised you survived your visit to Carlisle's. It's impressive, really."

"Where is she?"

"Not here. The boss took her yesterday." Clint tried to grin despite the swollen split in his lip. He was missing another tooth. "She was fun while it lasted."

Fury made the blood in Callum's veins pound. The thought of this cretin laying a single finger on Wynne was enough to make him see red. He knew Clint was baiting him, and damn him, but it was working.

"You look like shit. Who'd you piss off?"

"Ah, the boss took offense at my having a little fun with the goods."

Callum swallowed a growl. "And you took it out on another innocent? You sick bastard."

Clint chuckled. "I'd hardly call that whore an innocent."

Callum advanced towards the bed. The urge to shift and tear the other man's throat out was almost too much to contain. "Tell me what you've done with my friend, Clint, and maybe you'll still have balls left for fucking whores when I'm done with you."

"I told you, already. The boss took her. I don't know where. He doesn't tell me that kind of shit. Boss gives me a job; I do the job. Asking questions just pisses him off."

"This boss of yours have a name?"

"Pft, why should I tell you?"

Callum shifted. His prey yelped in surprise and Callum was on him before the man could scramble from the blankets, one heavy paw pressing him into the mattress. He brought his face down towards Clint's, clacking his teeth threateningly. Never had he felt the urge to murder a man in cold blood as he did now. It was a good thing he wasn't a wolf, but even if he was, Callum suddenly knew that he'd gladly trade this man's death for the moon madness.

"Okay, okay. Don't eat me," Clint squeaked. A sudden odor told Callum the man had pissed himself. "His name is Ainsley Crichton. He's some kinda fancy lord. Calls himself Lord Windholt."

Callum shifted smoothly back to a man. "Where are his estates?"

"How the fuck should I know? Do I look like a governess to you?"

"I thought you didn't want to die?"

Clint's jaw clicked shut and Callum backed away.

"I swear to you and all the stars in the ten heavens, if I don't find her whole and hale, I will hunt you down and rip you limb from limb. And if she tells me you laid a single putrid finger on her, there is nowhere in this miserable world that you will be able to hide from me. Do we have an understanding?"

Clint nodded weakly.

Callum grunted and headed for the door. When he opened it, Ailsa was standing on the other side, wide-eyed and hugging herself. The sight of her, frightened and bruised, rekindled his fury.

"And Clint?" he said, looking back over his shoulder at the man. "I'll be coming back through here on my way home. If you put another mark on any one of these ladies, I'll put you in the ground just the same."

The woman in scarlet—whom Callum now suspected was the Madam—was still sitting on the chaise when Callum stomped out of the brothel. She glanced at him, the smoke dribbling upward from her pursed lips.

"Who is Ainsley Crichton?"

She expelled the rest of the smoke on a heavy sigh. "You really are jumping in with both feet. I hope the girl is worth it."

"She is."

The madam eyed him a long moment, tapping the ashes out of her pipe into a small bowl. "I am proud to say I have never needed a man to protect me. I've done a pretty damn good job of that myself. However, some of those girls in there." She jerked her perfectly coifed head towards the door. "They could've used someone who believed they were worth it.

"Ainsley Crichton is a rich sonofabitch who makes his money dealing in everything illegal, from mundane drugs to black magics. He bought up some land a week's ride north of here a few years ago and styled himself as a lord. Rumor is, he got himself a real title from the king, for all the good that's worth."

"Thank you."

Her regard went from searching to stern. "Don't thank me. I just sent you to your death, stupid boy."

In which Goldilocks finds an ally

The carriage rattled on for hours and Wynne found herself dozing off out of sheer boredom—impressive when one considered the long nap the magic had imposed on her. Her captor didn't speak to her again. Instead, he busied himself with a small, cheaply bound book that Wynne suspected might be an obscene novelette, judging by the way he kept adjusting himself. The only time he took notice of her was to rap her knuckles soundly with his cane when she dared to reach for the thick curtains covering the window.

"How can you read with so little light?" she groused, mostly because there was nothing better to say. "It's still daytime, we could be enjoying the sunshine."

"So you can examine the countryside? No, no, my dear, it won't do. Besides, I have *excellent* vision."

He went back to his book; Wynne went back to dozing.

It felt like she'd just managed to fall

completely asleep when the carriage finally ground to a halt. Wynne sat up, rubbing the sleep from her eyes. Daylight no longer leaked around the curtains, leaving the carriage interior grown pitch black. Wynne's heart rate accelerated. It was too dark and too small. Across from her, she could hear Windholt shuffling around, perhaps gathering his belongings.

"We should probably cover a few ground rules before we go inside," his voice said in the darkness.

Wynne strained her eyes, but she couldn't make out anything about what he was doing or his expression. She swallowed a moan of panic.

"If you are a good girl, you can stay upstairs with me in a nice, comfy bed," he continued, his voice sweet as honey before shifting into a hard, cruel edge. "But if you are not, I'm afraid you will have plenty more of this to look forward to in the cellar. Have I made myself clear?"

Wynne couldn't resist the whimper that rose up in her throat.

"That's what I thought." The carriage door popped open, and the silver light of the waning moon flooded the interior, illuminating the malicious smirk that cut across Windholt's face. "Come along now, my beauty. It's been a long day of travel and I am ready for a rest."

They stepped out onto a cobbled drive, in front of what appeared to be a modest manor house. Lights burned in the windows and smoke rose from several of its many chimneys, the ghostly plumes gray against the velvet sky.

"Where are we?" Wynne demanded.

"Tut, tut. No questions, lovely. Come now, we mustn't keep our hosts waiting. It's rude."

Windholt led her up the wide staircase to the great double doors. They were lacquered in a garish red with far too much gold leafing. A great wolf's head was carved in relief above it, jaws open and snarling. It gave Wynne shivers that had nothing to do with the cool night air.

A well-dressed servant met them at the door. "Welcome, milord. His Lordship is expecting you," the man —a butler or steward, Wynne guessed—said in a gravelly voice. "Dinner will be served at half past."

"Excellent, excellent. That's just enough time to freshen up. The usual rooms?"

"They have been aired out for you, my lord. Shall I escort you, sir?"

Windholt waved him off. "No need; I know the way. Come, my lovely. I'm sure you'll find our accommodations quite pleasant."

Wynne shot the butler a pleading look, which he pointedly ignored. She had to bite her lip to keep her mouth shut. She had to lull Windholt into a false sense of security if she was ever going to have any chance of getting away from him.

The hallways of the manor house were sparsely lit, with lamps in sconces set too many feet apart. Flickering flames struggled against an oppressive darkness that seemed to ooze from every corner. A sense of dread crept under Wynne's skin, and she had to resist the urge to scratch at her arms. Windholt strode confidently through the gloom, seemingly unfazed. Wynne struggled to keep up in her much-too-big slippers.

The wolf motif from the front door continued in the paintings and tapestries that lined the halls. Most depicted noble beasts in their natural forest environment, but a few of them turned Wynne's stomach. One featured a giant wolf ripping out the throat of a man in hunter's garb. Another featured a pack taking down a large bear that looked too much like Callum for Wynne's peace of mind.

Windholt stopped before a pair of gilded doors on the second floor. He shoved them open with great theatrics, ushering Wynne inside. Like the hallways, the chamber was inadequately lit, but she got the impression of dark wood, heavy drapes, and thick carpets.

"Forswraithe and I have a standing arrangement. When I stay at Green Briar, I am afforded the use of this fine suite of rooms."

"They seem... lovely." In truth, she suspected that daylight would reveal the rooms to be gaudy and tasteless, but she knew such remarks would only draw his ire. If luck was on her side, Wynne wouldn't have to see the rooms in enough light to prove her hypothesis. Her captor had finally slipped up and given her a clue about her whereabouts. She'd never heard of Green Briar or this Forswraithe, but it was a start.

Windholt moved through the shadowy sitting room to a door that Wynne assumed led to the bed chamber. She stayed rooted to the spot. No way in hell was she going anywhere near a bed while that man was in the room. He wasn't overtly threatening in the way men like Clint were, but she'd seen the glint in his eyes. Windholt wasn't above abusing her that way. In fact, he was probably a sicker bastard than twenty Clints combined.

Thankfully, Windholt didn't seem to care whether she freshened up before dinner or not. He reemerged from the bedchamber in a different waistcoat and jacket, his hair slicked back with fresh pomade.

"On to dinner then," he announced, offering her his arm.

Wynne was loath to touch him, but when she hesitated a thundercloud rolled up in his gray eyes. She quickly looped her arm with his and the storm passed, a sunny smile lighting up his face.

Like much of the house she'd seen so far, the dining room was trying to be elegant but had overshot and landed somewhere in the vicinity of garish. The wallpaper, she noted, once again featured a wolf motif, as did the carved backs of the chairs.

Three people were already seated at the dining table. Two women sat to the left-hand side of the table head. One was young and pretty, dressed in a fine gown of seafoam green silk. She had a face that looked like it was made for smiles and laughter, and yet she sat quiet and subdued, staring at her empty place setting. Next to her sat a stately older woman who bore enough resemblance to the girl that Wynne assumed she must be her mother. She wore the expression of someone who had just sucked on a lemon.

It was the man at the head of the table who made shivers run down her spine. Although he was elegantly dressed in the latest fashions, there was no hiding his savage nature. Something wolfish in his smirk reminded her of Bleddyn. This man was a werebeast—she was sure of it. Unlike Bleddyn, no good humor lit this man's golden eyes. There was only wild hunger.

"Lord Windholt, I'm so glad you could join us," the man said, rising and rounding the table. He spoke to Ainsley, but his eyes never left Wynne. "And who is this delightful creature you've brought with you?"

"Ah, Lord Green Briar, it is my distinct pleasure to introduce you to my lovely Goldie. Goldie, this is Lord Gethin Forswraithe of Green Briar."

"The pleasure is all mine, I'm sure," the baron said, lifting Wynne's bare free hand to his lips. She felt her heart rate soar. He grinned at her, showing off pronounced canines. It was probably for the best that her inner well was filled with Callum's curse, because in that moment she might have yanked Forswraithe's gift right out of him from sheer terror. No doubt he knew exactly what she was, and by taking her hand, he was informing her that he held no fear of her ability.

"Please, join us." He gestured to the table.

"I'm sure you recall my lovely wife, Elain, and my daughter, Mared."

Elain nodded towards them, but her sour expression did not change. Mared continued her study of the flatware.

Windholt steered Wynne towards the seat across from the younger woman before seating himself at Forswraithe's right hand.

The conversation between the two men was cordial through the first few courses. They discussed mutual acquaintances and business interests while the wine flowed freely. The women, by contrast, ate in perfect silence.

Wynne picked at her food, moving it around with her fork and attempting to make it look like she'd consumed something. Once, she caught the gaze of the girl across the table. Pale amber eyes widened, then immediately retreated. There would be no help from that quarter, Wynne supposed.

"So, this is the girl that played your man for a fool, or you settled on a different sort of conquest?"

"This is the one. She's usually quite lively, aren't you, lovely?" Windholt said, patting her knee.

Wynne felt her lip curl of its own volition. "Quite."

Forswraithe chuckled. "I have to admit, I've never seen such a lovely siphon witch before. Usually they're so... ugly."

At the word siphon, Elain and Mared both jolted. Mared stared at Wynne in horror while Elain whirled on her husband.

"You let him bring a siphon in our house?"

she hissed. Her eyes darted to Mared and back to Forswraithe. "Are you insane?"

"I mean your daughter no harm," Wynne said, keeping her gaze locked with Mared's. "Whatever her gift may be, I have no interest in it. In fact, I have no interest in being here at all." She could feel Windholt's glare, but Forswraithe only laughed.

"You see?" Forswraithe said when his chuckles subsided. "Perfectly safe."

Skittish servants ducked in to whisk away their plates, replacing them with thick slices of a divine looking chocolate torte. Everyone except Wynne picked up their dessert forks.

"At least taste it, lass," Forswraithe said, pointing towards her plate with his fork. That feral gleam was in his eyes again. "One might think you don't appreciate my hospitality."

Windholt cut her another sharp glare. Clearly, he valued this arrangement. His expression promised retribution if she did anything to offend their host. Wynne picked up the fork with numb fingers and took a large bite of the cake. It sat heavy on her tongue like mud. She struggled to swallow. She had to force down several more bites before Windholt's attention shifted elsewhere. Forswraithe, however, was still watching her with a hungry expression.

When at last the meal was concluded, one of Windholt's men appeared to escort Wynne back to the guest quarters. She wasn't shocked to recognize the man who had helped Clint chase her into Callum's house. He at least had the decency to look discomforted by the whole situation.

"And see that she stays there," Windholt said, when the man started to lead Wynne away by her elbow. "Lord Green Briar and I have much business to discuss. I expect that we'll be quite late." He gave Wynne a lascivious smile. "Don't wait up, my beauty."

The second Arlo shut her in, Wynne began a thorough investigation of her new prison. Wynne wasn't about to share a bedroom with Ainsley Crichton. It was one thing to doze in the carriage and another thing entirely to share his bed. She doubted he'd let her avail herself of the floor or a chair though.

Although the windows lining the wall were tall and wide, they were too high off the ground to make for a viable escape route. Even if she had some rope, Wynne didn't think she'd actually be able to repel down the side of the building without falling. And even if she didn't break her neck, she doubted she'd just get up and walk away from such a tumble.

Pressing her ear to the crack between the doors, Wynne could make out the small sounds of Arlo standing watch outside. He wouldn't leave until Ainsley returned— maybe not even then.

Cursing softly, Wynne plopped onto one of the wingbacks by the hearth.

A scratching sound in the walls made

Wynne shudder. The manor looked to be well kept—if a bit dim—but looks could be deceiving. Were there rats in the walls? She hated rats. The idea of their little paws crawling over her and their whiskery noses brushing against her flesh made her want to vomit, never mind when they started to bite.

The rat in the wall turned out not to be a rat at all, but a wolf. Mared stepped out from behind one of the tapestries across the room, making Wynne jump.

"Shhh," Mared hissed, her pale eyes darting to the door and back to Wynne. She gestured for Wynne to come to her. When Wynne didn't move, the gestures became more frantic.

With a glance toward the door, Wynne rose quietly and tiptoed across the room.

"I assume you want to get out of here?" the girl whispered, her gaze searching Wynne's face for something. Ill-intent, perhaps?

"You have no idea how badly."

A small smile quirked the corners of Mared's lips. "Oh, I have a pretty good idea. Come on. These walls are full of tunnels."

Wynne followed the girl through a hole in the wall. Mared pulled a lever and the wall shifted silently back into place. Only a single lamp lit the narrow space. Once again, the familiar panic of cramped, dark spaces washed over Wynne, and she had to bite her lip to keep from whimpering.

"You'd never find these doors if you didn't know where to look," Mared assured her quietly, misinterpreting Wynne's unease.

"My great-great-grandfather was a paranoid bastard."

"Why are you helping me? Won't you father be angry when his guest's new toy disappears?"

"He is *not* my father," she spat. Her amber eyes flashed golden in the light of her lamp. "Just because he fucks my mother doesn't mean he has any claim to me. Gethin is my uncle and nothing more. He shouldn't even be Lord Forswraithe. My brother should be sitting in my father's chair."

"I don't—I don't do well in small, dark spaces," Wynne admitted, changing the subject. She was struggling to force herself to breathe normally. "The sooner we can get out of here, the better."

They crept sideways through spaces barely wide enough to allow them passage. Wynne couldn't imagine how a man built like Callum could be expected to squeeze through these tunnels. Maybe they weren't supposed to, and that was the point. Still, the feel of the timber and plaster closing in on her, scraping against her shoulder blades, nearly made her gasp. She found herself biting on her fist to keep the sounds of her panic muffled. Beyond the confines of this temporary torture, she could hear the sounds of the household staff going about their business.

Suddenly, Mared stopped, and Wynne bumped into her. The other girl grunted at the impact.

"Why did we stop?" Wynne asked, her voice coming out higher than she'd intended.

"We're going to be coming up on the most dangerous part of this adventure. Ahead is a ridiculously steep, narrow stairway. Once we get to the bottom of it, we must be absolutely silent while we pass by the drawing room. Otherwise, my uncle or his friend might hear us."

The steps—as narrow as the rest of the tunnel—were a harrowing experience. Wynne bit her lip until she tasted blood.

You're fine, Wynne. Just breathe, she told herself. *It's not like there isn't any light. Stars, I wish Callum was here.*

That thought brought her up short. Wynne hadn't wished for anyone since she was a child. When she'd cried for her mother, the traders had cruelly informed her of the woman's betrayal. That was the last time Wynne had cried out for anyone in fear or sadness. Now she found herself wishing for this man—barely more than a stranger—so he could dry her tears and hold her hand until the sky came back.

I might never see him again, she realized.

It brought a lump to her throat that had nothing to do with her fear of the dark. He wouldn't know what had happened to her. He might even assume that she'd ditched him—Wynne knew that would hurt him.

The floor—if you could call it that—at the bottom of the steps was dirt. Voices on the other side of the wall snapped Wynne out of her thoughts and a fresh wave of terror rolled over her. Windholt and Forswraithe—Gethin, Mared had called him—were laughing.

Wynne sucked in a breath and held it, not daring to so much as exhale as she and Mared crept by. She imagined the men were only feet away, oblivious to the subterfuge behind the wolf-printed wallpaper. Lath and plaster had never seemed so thin before.

Something in the uneven floor caught the toe of Wynne's too-big shoe. She pitched forward with a small gasp, bumping into Mared who very nearly dropped the lamp. Wynne hit the floor and the wolf girl whirled around in the small space to stare at her, eyes wide with fear.

Fuck.

In which plans go awry

So, what are your plans for the girl?" Forswraith asked, swirling the brandy in his glass as he spoke.

The two of them sat in the library with a decanter of brandy and a box of fat cigars. Ainsley took a sip of his drink to buy time as he considered the question. The Baron of Green Briar was a useful ally, but that didn't make him a trusted confidant.

"She's too pretty to just be put to market," Forswraith continued, flicking ash from his cigar. "Although perhaps a bit willful for my tastes. You can see the hate in her eyes." He grinned wolfishly. "And she *really* hates you."

"I believe I shall keep her for my personal collection," Windholt said at last, ignoring the barb. He reached for the decanter to top off his glass. "Siphons are infinitely useful, and my current asset is getting a bit..." He waved a hand dramatically, as if shifting the air for the right words. "Worn out."

Forswraithe chuckled. "You do seem to have that effect on women, Crichton."

Windholt waved that thought away. "No, no. As entertaining as I'm sure she will be in *that* capacity, I was referring to his gift. Overuse a siphon and they sort of—how do you describe it?—burn out. At least, he describes it as a burning sensation. I've had to resort to hiring out for a few jobs as of late. Having another siphon in my private stables seems prudent."

"Perhaps you ought to try breeding them," Gethin suggested.

Windholt shrugged. "It's not as if it hasn't been tried. Male siphons are *exceedingly* rare, but the few studies done on them suggest they may be infertile. There's no known cases of a male siphon producing any get, at any rate," he said, taking another sip of brandy.

"But the women do?"

"Produce get? Yes." He paused to take a long drag on his cigar. "But their offspring are almost never siphons. Still, it may be worth a try. Poor Gilvery deserves a reward after so many years of faithful service. Perhaps a tumble with a pretty siphon wench will raise his spirits."

They shared a chuckle before falling into companionable silence. Windholt found that he genuinely liked Forswraithe, which was rare. Most of his business associates were the sort of men one did not bring into polite company. The Baron of Green Briar wasn't exactly a cultured man—werewolves rarely were—but he was a pleasant and respectable enough fellow. His title was old and venerated, in any case.

Forswraithe sat up ramrod straight. "Did you hear that?" he mouthed. Windholt shook his head. Of all the gifts he had stolen with siphon magic, none of them had included particularly acute hearing.

"I almost forgot," Forswraithe said, perhaps a bit more loudly than was strictly necessary. "Those papers you wanted to see are in my office. We should deal with those before we turn in." The werewolf rose from his chair and stalked towards the door on silent feet, jerking his head to indicate that Windholt should go with him. Windholt shot him a puzzled expression but rose to follow.

When they were out in the hallway, Forswraithe closed the door to the library with a deliberate rattle. "There are rats in the walls," he muttered.

Windholt frowned. "Rats?"

"Big ones. Follow me."

Forswraithe led him through the familiar halls and stairway to his own chamber. Arlo, still standing watch as he'd been instructed, frowned slightly when he saw the lord of the manor, but bowed as elegantly as he could.

"Bring out the siphon girl," Forswraithe ordered.

Arlo glanced at Windholt, who nodded ever so slightly. Assured that he wouldn't suffer for it later, Arlo went in to retrieve the girl. He came out several seconds later, eyes wide in alarm.

"She's not here, milords. I—I don't understand." He'd gone pale under his tan. "I was right here the whole time. I would've seen her—"

Forswraithe grunted. "As I suspected. It seems my daughter is going through one of her rebellious periods. It's not your man's fault, Windholt. Mared wouldn't have used the door. Let's go, or we'll end up spending the whole night tracking them down."

"The property backs up to a dense wood," Arlo said, flinching when both lords turned to glare at him for speaking out of turn. "No disrespect, milords, but the girl disappeared into the woods once. I wouldn't put it past her to do so again."

Mared swore and Wynne jumped.

"I thought you said we have to be quiet!"

"No point now," Mared said, although she kept her voice low. She grabbed Wynne and put her mouth right against her ear. Her breath was hot and damp against Wynne's skin. "My uncle must have heard us. We can't go the way I was planning; he'll expect it. Stay close and keep your mouth shut."

She released Wynne and started creeping down the tunnel again.

They took so many turns that Wynne quickly lost track of where they might be in the manor. She didn't know the layout anyway, so perhaps trying to map it in her head had been a futile effort. Eventually, they emerged in what appeared to be a scullery.

"Where are we going?" Wynne demanded, catching ahold of Mared's sleeve.

"Shhh. You'll see." The girl slipped across the empty space like a wraith.

Wynne remained frozen in place, her eyes darting about the room. Supper wasn't that long ago. Why was the scullery empty? Shouldn't there be servants scrubbing pots and pans?

Mared looked behind and rolled her eyes before ghosting her way back to Wynne's side. "Don't worry," she whispered. "The servants are still supping. They won't be back for a candlemark or so. Now, come *on*."

The scullery had three doors—not counting the secret one in the wall—and Wynne assumed one led to the main kitchen and another into the pantries. The last door opened out to the back garden.

Mared led her through rows of early spring vegetables and herbs in raised beds. Leafy lettuces at their spring peak and the tops of carrots provided some cover under the crystalline light of the moon. Beyond the relative cover of the kitchen gardens, the estate's lawn rolled out like a bedspread, flat and exposed.

"I wanted to go straight to the stables," Mared explained when they were a good distance from the door. "But my uncle will expect that. Our best bet is to have you escape over the garden wall and through the woods at the back of the property. The other side of the woods is the end of my uncle's estate. If you can get through, you'll be out of his jurisdiction."

Wynne seriously doubted that Ainsley or Forswraithe gave a rat's ass about jurisdiction, but there was a more immediate problem with Mared's plan.

"We'll never make it without being seen," Wynne whispered. "Even if we do, your uncle is a wolf, isn't he? Won't he just track me down."

Mared flashed a grin as feral as any Wynne had seen from her werebeast acquaintances.

"It runs in the family. We just have to get you to the wall. I'll hold off whoever comes chasing after us long enough for you to get away."

"What about you?"

"Don't worry about me. Just make sure you hang on tight."

Before Wynne could blink, a large black wolf stood in the young woman's place, staring at her with the same amber eyes. Just a week ago Wynne would've hesitated, but now she leapt onto the werebeast's back without a second thought. Mared shot forward with a ground eating stride, forcing Wynne to cling desperately. She wrapped her arms tight about the wolf's neck, her face in the thick, silky coat.

They were halfway across the lawn when the alarm went up. The first shouts from the manor sent a shot of panic through Wynne, and she squeezed Mared's neck tighter. The wolf growled a warning. *You're choking me.*

It seemed to Wynne that they flew across the open ground. The next thing she knew, she was landing in the grass at Mared's feet as the wolf became a woman once again.

"Go!" Mared ordered, no longer bothering

to keep her voice low.

She laced her fingers together to form a stirrup with her hands, gesturing for Wynne to step up. With Mared's aid, Wynne was able to scramble up to the top of the sturdy stone wall.

"Come with me!" Wynne begged, straddling the wall with one hand held down for Mared to grasp.

The werewolf shook her head. "No time. Go!"

She shifted, effectively ending the argument. The wolf darted back the way they'd come, making a beeline for the pursuers sprinting from gardens.

"Good luck, Mared," Wynne whispered to the empty air. The backs of her eyes burned, threatening tears.

A hand wrenched her ankle downward.

Wynne screeched and clutched at the wall. Ainsley grabbed her wrist with his other hand, trying to pry her loose.

How did he know? she thought frantically.

"Leaving so soon, lovely? Don't you know it's poor manners to eat and run?" He grunted with effort, but Wynne clung to the wall like a leech, desperately flailing her leg, trying to dislodge his grip.

"You shouldn't have made me angry, foolish girl," he snarled. "Now we're going to have to do this the hard way."

Searing heat lit up every nerve ending where his hands gripped her flesh. "Just because I don't need my gifts to hurt you doesn't mean I won't use them," he growled. His burning fingers burrowed into her flesh, and Wynne screamed. She had to force him to let go. She had to—

With little thought for the consequences, Wynne opened up the channels of her gift, forcefully evicting the one curse she had.

It slammed into Windholt, nearly causing him to double over in pain. His grip on her loosened reflexively, and Wynne ripped her limbs away, falling backwards down the other side of the wall. She landed on her back, the air forced from her lungs. On the other side of the wall, Windholt was groaning.

"What did you do to me?" he demanded.

Wynne didn't answer. She rolled over and scrambled to her feet, hobbling and wheezing a bit before she got into the rhythm of running. One of her shoes had come off in the struggle and she kicked the other away.

"What did you do to me, you bitch?!"

No more than you deserve, Wynne thought, as Windholt's screams grew more frantic and distant.

He'd probably have another siphon remove the curse eventually, but for now she could take some satisfaction in knowing that Callum would never suffer from it again.

Everything hurt.

Wynne limped through the woods, doing her best not to feel sorry for herself. Escaping from her captor was no small feat and never would've been possible if not for Mared.

And Callum, she amended. Without his curse, she might not have gotten away even with Mared's help.

Although... perhaps if she'd had more time to think it through, she wouldn't have been so reckless about using the curse. Force expelling it all at once like that was essentially giving herself siphoning sickness on purpose. Her head pounded in time with the roiling sensation in her stomach. She itched where the channels of her gift ran underneath her skin, like lines of rug-burn embedded deep in her flesh. Adrenaline had kept her running until it ran out and the symptoms overwhelmed her.

Exhaustion and siphoning sickness weren't her only problems. The skin of her right wrist and ankle was red and angry. Black marks clearly outlined where Ainsley's fingertips had dug into her.

What the hell kind of gift did he steal? she wondered.

Something sharp bit into the sole of her foot and Wynne stifled a scream. She hopped one-legged to a tree, supporting herself with one hand while using the other to wrestle her skirts out of the way. Blood stained the bottom of her left stocking; she'd driven something into the tender arch of her abused foot.

Sobs she couldn't contain rose in her throat. Wynne sank to the ground, tears streaming down her face. She clasped both hands over her mouth, trying to muffle the sounds of her despair. Windholt wouldn't give up looking for her, and there were surely men in the woods hunting for her right this very instant.

Pull yourself together, Wynne.

Tearing strips out of her skirts for bandages was more difficult than trashy novelettes made it sound. She bound her bleeding foot as best she could, then bound the other one just to provide it with some sliver of protection more than her stockings offered. The dirtiest part of the skirt at the bottom she used to tie up the remaining fabric in a big knot at her rear. She didn't want to leave anything behind, but the voluminous skirt was not ideal for fleeing through the forest.

Fresh tears pricked her eyes when she put weight on her injured foot, but she bit her lip and hobbled a few steps.

Keep moving, she told herself. *Don't stop. Stopping is dying.*

A distant howl split the night, followed by a braying chorus of hounds. A fresh jolt of terror shot through Wynne. Searching men she might evade in the dark but not hunting dogs.

Pain assaulted her as she ran. The underbrush tore at her clothes and tree branches grasped for her hair. The air in her lungs burned like fire.

Just get out of the woods, Wynne. You can find help if you get out of the woods.

Ahead, the trees began to thin, and her heart soared. Flickering light that might be cottage windows danced through the foliage.

Wynne burst from the tree line and into a small clearing. A tidy cottage surrounded by rose bushes sat at its center, bathed in moonlight. A woman in a dark cloak spun around from the plant she'd been tending, a crossbow held at the ready.

"Please." Wynne was gasping, struggling for the air to form the words. Darkness swam at the edges of her vision. "Please don't let them—"

"Whoa, hey. Don't you pass out on me." The woman glanced around before raising her voice in a shout that Wynne was sure would split her aching head in two. "Grandmother! Grandmother, come quick!"

Wynne had the vague impression of silver hair before exhaustion finally claimed her.

In which Baby Bear finds a clue

Have you seen a pretty blonde woman? About this tall." Callum held up a hand even with his collarbone. "Hazel eyes, freckles. Possibly in a state of partial undress?"

"I can't say that I have, son," the farmer said, leaning against his hoe. His bushy gray eyebrows drew together in concern. "Why?"

"My friend went missing in Wickersburg and I suspect it wasn't voluntarily."

The farmer shook his head. "I'm sorry I can't be of more help."

Callum struggled to keep his desperation in check. He'd lost count of the farms he'd passed since leaving Wickersburg. Nobody anywhere had seen Wynne or anyone even vaguely matching her description, and Callum didn't know what this Windholt looked like. He regretted not asking Clint or the madam more questions, but it was too late now. If he wasted time doubling back to Wickersburg, he might never find Wynne.

"You haven't seen anything suspicious?"

Callum asked, changing tactics. "Nothing at all?"

"What's suspicious? All sorts of strange folks travel the King's Roads."

The King's Roads were a network of wide, cobbled trade routes maintained by the Crown. The road north out of Wickersburg was one of them, and the farmer had a fair point. A lot of people passed by on such roads and many of them would seem strange to provincial farmers in this far-flung end of the kingdom.

"What about nobility? Have you seen anyone who looked like they might be a lord or a wealthy landowner? Maybe a fancy carriage?"

"No—"

"Papa!" a shrill voice called from the farmhouse's door. "Papa, what about that man?"

The farmer sighed heavily. "Imogen, I told you to let that go."

A young woman with straw-colored hair and a scowl marched towards them. Her skin was red from too many hours laboring in the sun, and the deep furrows in her forehead suggested her scowl was a permanent feature.

When she was close enough to speak without shouting, she glared at her father and said, "It was a mighty strange request, Papa, and if you won't tell him, I will."

"Imogen, how many times have I told you not to eavesdrop?"

She rolled her eyes. "Yesterday afternoon, a strange man came to the door. He asked

Mama if he could buy the nicest dress we owned. I was out in the field at the time and didn't know what was happening. I never would've let Mama sell my only fancies had I known. But lo-and-behold, I come in from toiling out in the fields with him," —she jerked a thumb in her father's direction— "and come to find out Mama sold them to some random stranger."

"What did he look like?"

"I didn't get a good look. Only saw him from a distance, but the carriage he came with looked real fancy." She turned back towards the house and hollered, "Mama! Mama, get out here! This man wants to know about that bastard who bought my fancies!"

The screeching made Callum wince, but he bit his tongue. This was the first clue he'd had since leaving town. It might turn out to be nothing, but until he knew for sure, he couldn't risk offending this odious young lady.

"Mama, tell him about the man who bought my fancies," Imogen demanded when her mother finally joined them. The woman looked like Callum felt with his curse.

"He wasn't particularly remarkable," she said, folding her stick-thin arms. "Maybe a bit slender. His eyes were kind of small. He didn't seem a fancy lady's servant, but he said he needed a dress for his employer's mistress. There was some sort of accident, and they lost her luggage or some such. I didn't pay attention too much after he started jingling that fat coin purse of his."

Callum glanced at Imogen, trying to appraise her form without appearing to do so. Her frame was somewhat similar to Wynne's. They were about the same height and their shoulders were probably the same width, but where Wynne was all luscious curves, Imogen was flat as a board. Still, given that all of Wynne's belongings were in Callum's possession, it seemed likely that the dress was for her.

"Can you tell me which way the carriage went?"

"They turned left at the crossroads by Old Man Haggard's farm," Imogen said, jumping in before either of her parents could respond. "I know, because once Mama told me what she'd done, I tried to chase 'em down."

"Foolish girl," the farmer muttered.

"Where does that road lead?"

"Green Briar," father and daughter said in unison.

"Thank you." Callum hurried to pull some coins from his pocket. He pressed them into Imogen's boney hands. "This was very helpful!"

Before any of them could respond, Callum took off at a run, his body melting into bear form. Behind him, he could hear the farming family gasp. It was a risk, taking this form on the road in broad daylight, but he could move faster this way. Either way, his legs still felt like lead.

I'm coming, Wynne, he thought. *I'm coming.*

The village attached to the Green Briar estate was a tidy little town. It was larger than Snoaksly-on-Barnham—although not by much. But like Snoaksly-on-Barnham, it appeared to be the sort of place where everybody knew everybody, and the presence of a stranger like Callum was sure to be noted. He could practically feel the gaze of curious eyes as he strolled into town with two packs slung over his back.

It seemed that the stars were smiling on his venture because it was market day. Several wooden stalls at one end of the village square were doing a brisk business selling the produce of early spring, leafy greens and sweet peas, amongst other things. The smell wafting from the baker's display made his stomach rumble. Callum heeded the grumbling complaints and headed for the stall. Spending some coin might be a good way to loosen some lips, too. Two birds, one stone—as the saying went.

Although the line for the baker was long, it moved quickly. Soon there was just one tiny old woman between him and the round-faced girl selling crusty loaves and sweet sticky buns that made his mouth water.

"Edna!" the baker's assistant exclaimed. "Was something wrong with the bread Rowan picked up this morning?"

The old woman shook her head. "No, no, nothing like that. A mouse got into it already.

I told Rowan we need to set traps, but, soft-hearted thing that she is, the girl begged me not to."

"Rowan? Soft-hearted?" the baker's assistant snorted. "I'll believe that when pigs fly. What can I get for you?"

Callum tuned out of the conversation when they started haggling, as he had with all the conversations before that. If anyone knew anything about Wynne, they weren't talking about it with the baker's assistant. Something that felt suspiciously like anxiety twisted his gut. Was Wynne okay? Had the Siphoning Sickness hit her yet?

It had occurred to him on the way to Green Briar that Wynne had been holding his curse for several days at this point. The idea of her getting sick because of him filled him with shame. The idea of her getting sick while held captive by a man like Ainsley Crichton made him furious. There was one thought he wouldn't allow himself though, for fear it would paralyze him—what would happen to Wynne if there was no one to absorb the curse when it finally demanded release?

"What can I do for you?" the baker's assistant asked.

The question snapped Callum out of his reverie. His stomach twisted, now rebelling at the mere suggestion of food. "Uh, two sticky buns."

"One pence."

Callum dug around in his coin purse and produced a shilling. "I'm afraid I'll have to overpay," he said, sliding it across the stall's counter. "But perhaps you could tell me something in exchange."

The young woman rolled her eyes. "Look mister, whatever sly trick you think you're going to pull to get up m' skirts isn't going to work. Especially not for a few fractions of a shilling."

Callum's face heated.

"N-no, it's nothing like that. I'm looking for someone. I was hoping maybe you'd seen her."

"Oh." It was the bakery assistant's turn to blush. "Right, sorry. Who is it?"

"I'm looking for a blonde woman about this tall." He held his hand at his collarbone. "She has hazel eyes and—"

"You and every other man in the village," she laughed. "I know His Lordship put a bounty on her head, but I didn't think word had spread much beyond Green Briar yet."

"A bounty?"

His confusion must have shown on his face, because she stopped laughing and studied him curiously.

"Oh. I thought you were one of the hunters looking for the thief that escaped from Green Briar last night. She was supposed to stand trial this morning but managed to get loose somehow." She leaned across the counter and whispered conspiratorially. "Rumor is, the lord's own step-daughter was involved in the jailbreak."

Callum's heart soared and he didn't know whether to laugh or cry. Wynne had escaped, which meant the siphoning sickness hadn't hit her while she was in Windholt's clutches.

He still had to find her to take back his curse, but at least he wouldn't have to break her out of the manor house to do it. The search for her wasn't going well if Windholt and his cronies had resorted to telling tall tales to rope the local populace into it. Unless there just happened to be another beautiful, blond thief running around the immediate countryside. Somehow, Callum doubted it.

"This bounty—how much is it?" he asked. It would be best to appear interested in the reward if he was going to pursue this line of questioning further.

"Fifty pounds."

It was a staggering amount of money. With that kind of reward on the table, every able-bodied man in the county would be on the hunt.

"That's a tempting prize for a game of hide and seek."

"They say the girl is like a ghost or a wood nymph." She shook her head as if she didn't quite believe the story herself. "Once she disappears into a forest, there's no finding her, apparently. His lordship had half the town in the woods looking for her last night. Even the dogs lost the scent."

Callum did his best to show her a careless smirk. "Well perhaps I shall do better."

She laughed and shot him a wink. "Yes, and when you do, come back here and buy me a drink."

Maybe if I'd met you a couple weeks ago, Callum thought. *You're pretty, but you're not Wynne.*

"I jest. I'm not much of a bounty hunter, I'm afraid. Just looking for work. The girl I'm looking for is my dimwitted cousin. Hardly criminal material."

"Ah. Well, I'm afraid no one else fitting your cousin's description has come through here, but if you're serious about looking for work, you might try the manor house. Last I heard, they were looking for stable hands again."

He thanked her for the information and the baked goods, hustling out the way of the restless patrons queuing up behind him. It only took a few minutes to wolf down the buns and lick his sticky fingers clean. Instinct urged him to run off into the woods immediately in search of Wynne's scent, but his better judgement smothered the impulse. Curious eyes were still following him and if he took off right away, he might risk leading the enemy right to her.

So, Callum lingered, feigning interest in the market and making small talk. The story he told was completely fabricated, of course, expounding on his lie to the bakery assistant about looking for work. Now that he knew the situation, he would have to do damage control and convince as many people as possible that he wasn't interested in the bounty or any blonde women except a wayward cousin who hadn't arrived yet.

The townsfolk happily filled him in on all the details of Wynne's escape without any prompting on his part. It seemed this was the most exciting event to visit itself upon the village in several years. Everyone was talking about it and dreaming of what they'd do if they caught her and earned the bounty.

"You'd never catch me working another day, I'll tell you that," the blacksmith said. He clapped Callum on the shoulder. "It was good to meet you, Brodie, but I had best get back to the forge before the missus comes looking for me. Stop by the shop later if you don't get that stable job. I have a few odd jobs that'll at least earn you a place to sleep and a bite to eat."

Callum smiled and agreed, inwardly chuckling at himself for giving his brother's name.

With a cover story established, Callum made his way towards the manor. It was set away from the village upon a small rise. A cobbled road led down from the grand estate, terminating at one corner of the village square. Trees shaded the road and partially blocked the house from view. Or, more likely, blocked the view of the village from the house.

It was simple enough for Callum to slip into the trees when he thought no one was looking. An eerily familiar scent was in the air. Callum breathed deeply, frowning. Then he shifted, enjoying the shimmer of magic that ran through him as his body swiftly reordered itself. Instantly his sense of smell became sharper, the odor practically punching him in the snout.

Werewolf.

The scent markings of a territorial werewolf were an unexpected development, and Callum wasn't sure what to make of it.

Usually, where there was one werewolf, there were many; Bleddyn was an unusual specimen in that regard. He was cursed outcast—shunned. But Callum hadn't noticed any werewolf scents in the village, which meant—

What the hell have I gotten myself into? he wondered.

He set off at a lumbering trot anyway, weaving between the trees and working his way around the manor house's grounds in a wide arc. His reconnaissance suggested that Wynne had escaped at the back of the property, disappearing into the dense woods behind it.

If he'd been human, Callum would've wept when he picked up the first hint of Wynne's scent. It was strongest where he found a sharp stick stained with dried blood. In it, he could smell her pain and fear. Rage burned in his gut. He would make sure Wynne was safe and then he would rid the world of Ainsley Crichton. No one else would suffer at that bastard's hand or by his orders.

The scent trail went on and on.

Until it didn't.

Callum stopped, dumbfounded. Just like it had at the Bird and Blue, Wynne's scent just... stopped. No wonder the hounds had lost the scent. It was clear magic was at work again for it to have disappeared so completely. There was no body of water for her to enter and come out somewhere else and unless she'd made friends with some sort of avian shifter in the last two days, she hadn't been plucked up into the sky. That only left masking magic.

Wynne can't use magic. Which means someone else got to her first. Damn it. He let out a huff of frustration. This practically put him back at square one—a day behind and no idea where to look next.

Callum continued straight in the direction Wynne had been heading. He didn't have any reason to believe she kept going straight ahead after her scent disappeared, but he could hope. It seemed she'd been running blindly in a fairly straight line, so it seemed like his best option. His only option. And he could always circle back and start again.... if he had to.

"You look like shit."

Windholt glared at Forswraithe over his morning tea but didn't deny the observation. The costly glass mirror in his chambers had told him the same story already. Ugly purple bags had already started to form under his eyes after a single sleepless night. Whatever the little siphon bitch had done, he was going to make her undo it the second he got his hands around that swan-neck of hers.

"My men are scouring the woods, as are yours. They'll find the lass. It's only a matter of time," Forswraithe assured him, misreading the cause of Windholt's discomposure.

"And what of your niece?"

A hot flush crept over Forswraithe's cheeks, but Windholt was too tired and too annoyed to care. They both knew Mared wasn't Forswraithe's get. Furthermore, they were both keenly aware that everything Forswraithe had—and that included his brother's willful daughter—he owed to Ainsley.

"She will be dealt with."

"I don't know what you have planned for the girl," Windholt said. He paused to take a purposefully dramatic sip of his tea before continuing. "And frankly, I don't care. But I expect you to control the chit better in the future. This whole fiasco is a waste of time and money. This is your mess, Forswraithe. Clean it up."

If looks could kill, Windholt was sure they'd be planning his funeral. He made it a point to ignore the werewolf's glare, focusing instead on his morning correspondence until the other man gave up and left the room. The moment the door slammed shut, Windholt pushed the paperwork aside and beckoned Arlo out of the shadows.

"How goes the search in truth?" Ainsley asked.

"We lost her," the wereweasel said without preamble. "The dogs lost the scent. She's probably cleared the woods by now."

Windholt frowned. The way she'd released whatever magic she'd been hiding was explosive and desperate. In his experience, careless siphons who didn't manage the flow of energy correctly always got sick, their condition deteriorating rapidly following the event. He seriously doubted she could get very far in that condition. No, she'd gone to ground somewhere, and these incompetent idiots had missed it.

"Keep searching. Something tells me she's still in there."

Arlo's expression was neutral, but Windholt knew him well enough to know he found that statement dubious at best. Unlike that idiot, Clint, however, Arlo was smart enough to keep that opinion to himself.

"Is there anything else, Arlo?"

"Yes, sir. One of the Hardy triplets is here. He says he and one of his brothers tracked the werebear here."

"Ah yes, our Goldie's stalwart bodyguard. Such devotion." Although he smiled dismissively, Windholt seethed inside. They did not need another complication. "Is it safe to assume that the other cat is tracking our ursine friend?"

"Yes, sir."

"Good. I want him dead this time. I think my quarters here could use a new rug, don't you? I'll double their usual fee."

"I doubt that will be necessary, sir. Liam Hardy died before his brothers left Wickersburg. This has become a personal matter for them."

"I see. Offer my condolences if you would, please." He didn't give a rat's ass about Liam Hardy, but cordiality was rarely a misstep in such matters.

"Of course, sir." The wereweasel bowed and was about to make his exit when a thought occurred to Ainsley.

"Wait. I've changed my mind. Tell them just to follow him for now and report back his movements."

"Sir?"

"He might lead us to the girl. After all, that's what he came all this way for, is it not?"

"And if he does? What are your orders, sir?"

Windholt just managed to retain his dignity and refrain from rolling his eyes. "*Then* they kill him and take the girl alive, you dolt."

Once again, Arlo maintained that polite, stoic expression that fooled no one. The wereweasel's fear of the werebear obviously far outweighed his confidence in the Hardy brothers' ability as hired muscle. Windholt let it go. Even those idiots couldn't manage to screw it up a second time. That bear was as good as dead.

In which Baby Bear is Trespassing

Waking up in places she didn't remember falling asleep was starting to become a habit, and Wynne wasn't sure she liked that. The ceiling above her was wholly unfamiliar with bundles of drying herbs and braids of garlic hung everywhere. Without moving too much to give away that she was awake, Wynne groped around carefully with her fingers. She was in a bed. A clean bed, from the scent of roses lingering on the sheets.

"There's breakfast if you're feeling up to it."

Wynne turned her head towards the voice. A willowy brunette was frowning at her from the doorway across the room, which appeared to be the interior of a tiny cottage. Morning sunlight streamed through the windows, bringing out hints of auburn in her dark hair. She unslung a crossbow from her back and propped it up against the wall before removing her dark red cloak.

"Where am I?" Wynne asked.

With her pretense of sleep nullified, she sat up and looked around openly. The wide bed was pushed against the back wall of the cottage. The only other furniture was a long table and bench before the oversized stone hearth to the right. Shelves lined the wall to the left.

"My bed," the stranger said. "Grandmother insisted we hide you." She stared at Wynne with humorless dark eyes. "My name is Rowan. Who are you and why are Forswraithe's men after you?"

"You can call me Goldie." Wynne winced as she spoke. She *really* had to think of a better alias. "And it's Windholt who wants me. Forswraithe is just his lapdog."

Rowan's frown deepened. It appeared that the name Windholt was not unknown to her. Wynne expected more questions, but Rowan changed the subject abruptly. "Stay put while I get you some porridge. If you undo all her doctoring, Grandmother will be angry." A small smirk played at her lips. "Mostly at me."

The porridge was hot and flavorful, sweetened with maple syrup and studded with raisins. Wynne's stomach grumbled when the scent hit her nose. It seemed she'd been out cold long enough for her stomach to settle because she was suddenly ravenous.

"So," Rowan said as she pulled up a stool to sit at Wynne's bedside, "what did you do to incur Windholt's wrath?"

"Exist," Wynne said between bites.

Rowan snorted and folder her arms. "Windholt doesn't want people without a reason. He wastes no time on anything doesn't make him money. Considering the time and energy he's spending on this manhunt, you must be very valuable to him."

The porridge on Wynne's tongue suddenly seemed like tasteless glue. She struggled to finish the bite before setting the spoon back in the bowl and holding it out towards her host. "I'm not hungry anymore."

Rowan refused the bowl. "Eat it all or Grandmother will have my hide."

Wynne sighed and took another bite. There wasn't much to chew, but it at least gave her a reason to delay speech while she debated with herself. She had no idea who Rowan was or what her relationship to Forswraithe or Windholt might be. It seemed Rowan and this mysterious Grandmother had protected Wynne from her pursuers, but that didn't mean they wouldn't turn on her once they knew the truth.

"We have no intention of turning you over to them for a bounty, if that's what you're worried about," Rowan put in when the silence stretched on for too long.

"You already have it mostly right," Wynne said. It wouldn't hurt to confirm what little of her suspicions Rowan had already divulged. "Windholt thinks he can make a lot of money by forcing me to use my gifts to his or his clients' advantage."

"And what would those gifts be exactly?"

Wynne dug into the porridge, ignoring the question. It was too much to hope Rowan would take the hint.

"Look, I don't really care what you can do," Rowan said when it became clear Wynne wasn't going to clarify any further without additional prodding. "I just want to know exactly how valuable Windholt thinks you are and how much danger you've brought to my grandmother's doorstep."

"Windholt likely considers me invaluable. Although I'm worth more to him alive than dead, it wouldn't surprise me if he killed me just to keep me from falling into a rival's hands."

"You think an awful lot of yourself, don't you?"

"*No.*" The word came more sharply than Wynne intended. "I've just met enough men like Windholt to know how they think. They see stacks of gold in place of living beings."

Rowan snorted and rose to her feet. "Keep your secrets, then. You won't be able to stay here long anyway. Forswraithe's men may fear my grandmother as a witch, but I doubt Windholt's minions will be so deterred."

"I should leave." Wynne tried to rise from the bed, but Rowan put a staying hand on her shoulder, pressing her back down.

"Wait. Grandmother will want to check you over first. She'll be back from the market soon. Rest until then."

"Why are you helping me? Not, not that I'm not grateful—" Wynne rushed to explain when Rowan's expression darkened. "But my troubles aren't yours, and these are dangerous men."

"Because Grandmother said so. If you

want to know her reasoning, you'll have to ask her. The stars above know we don't need any trouble from petty lords and their enforcers. Now, do you want more porridge before I get back to my chores?"

The cool shade of the trees eventually gave way to a clearing. Callum stopped at the tree line, observing the scene before him. Someone had built a garden in the middle of the woods. Raised and tiered beds of herbs and leafy spring greens lorded over a flower garden just coming alive with a riot of spring's favorite colors. White gravel formed walkways between them, shaded by lattices that would surely hold cucumbers and other vining things later in the season.

Callum ambled across the untamed grasses that encircled the garden. It was an island of ordered perfection amidst a sea of nature's chaos. He inhaled deeply, enjoying the mingled aromas of the flowers and all the fresh edible things. The scents of two human women lingered in the garden, but neither of them was Wynne. Odors he could only attribute to magic also clung to the place. This was a witch's garden.

Tread carefully, Callum, he thought. *You don't need to incur another witch's curse before you even find the first one. Stars above, what punishment would this lot think of if they thought you were stealing from them?*

Something slammed into his upper foreleg and Callum bellowed in surprise and pain. He staggered, pawing blindly at whatever had struck him. A crossbow bolt tore from his flesh and landed on the gravel, his blood turning the white stone scarlet.

Fuck.

Gravel crunched as his assailant closed in him. Callum looked up to find a woman in red bearing down on him, another bolt at the ready. He moaned at her, as much in pain as in warning, but fought the ursine instinct to tear her apart. Instead, he did the most un-bearlike thing he could imagine in the situation and just lay down on the gravel.

It had the intended effect, and the woman advanced. From the corner of his eye, Callum could see her expression was perplexed. He closed his eyes and let the transformation take him.

His attacker let out a yelp of surprise when her prey went from hairy to human in the blink of an eye. "Stars burn it, what is a werebear doing in my grandmother's garden?"

"Getting shot, apparently," Callum said through gritted teeth. In human form, the gravel was distinctly uncomfortable and the gushing hole in his bicep hurt like a bitch. "Are you going to shoot me again or help me up?"

She pointed the crossbow at his head. "Being human doesn't mean you aren't a predator."

"I swear upon the stars of my birth that I am not interested in eating you or your vegetables. I'm just looking for a friend and the trail led me here."

"A friend?" She seemed to relax for a moment, but then the weapon was aimed right at his face again. Her eyes narrowed. "What sort of friend?"

"Why don't you let me stanch the bleeding in my shoulder and I'll tell you?"

"You seem to be confused about who has the power here, Bear."

"Or maybe I just don't want to bleed to death while you enjoy your little power trip," he snapped. "Now, I'm going to sit up, and I'm going to stop my arm bleeding. You can either let me do that or shoot me again. Your choice."

The crossbow didn't waver, but she nodded, and Callum took that as good enough. He pushed himself into a sitting position with his good arm. Hissing in pain, he dropped both packs from his back and began the torturous process of removing his shirt. The right arm and shoulder of the garment was soaked through with his blood, the scarlet stark against the white linen. Callum bunched it up and pressed a dry portion to the new hole in his body.

"Damn lucky all you hit was muscle," he groused.

"The next shot won't be so lucky for you," the woman promised. "You've done what you wanted, now tell me what you're doing trespassing in our garden."

"I was following a trail. A friend of mine is missing and I'm afraid she's in trouble."

Callum watched the small, fleeting

expressions that marked her face as he spoke. Recognition. Suspicion.

Finally, she nodded. "Very well. If you're telling the truth, then you will live. If I find out you're lying—" she paused, her raven eyebrows arched, "—then I shall finish what I started." She gestured with the crossbow, indicating that Callum should stand up. "You will walk ahead of me so I can keep an eye on you."

He staggered to his feet and was surprised by a rush of wooziness. In truth, he was still a bit anemic from the fight with those werecats. He swayed on his feet for a moment before collapsing, barely able to catch himself before his face hit the gravel. He heard his captor curse and looked up to see her stalking towards him. There was a graceful economy of motion to her strides that made Callum wonder just which one of them was actually the predator.

"Fragile flower, aren't you?"

"You *shot* me," he protested. "And I've already lost too many pints of blood this week." The world was starting to get hazy. "Please. Help me." His words were starting to slur. He shook his head, trying to clear it. "I have to find her. Wynne—"

Rowan stared at the bleeding man passed out in her grandmother's garden. One second he'd been speaking, and the next his eyes had rolled up in his head.

"Hey," she said, prodding him none too gently with the toe of her boot. "Hey, wake up. Hey! I can't carry you, you great lummox."

He didn't stir.

Stars, burn it all to ashes, she thought. *I should just leave him here and send someone for the body.*

The image of his pleading eyes before they rolled up into his head flashed across her memory. He'd seemed so sincere.

Damn it all, Rowan. This is not the time to be getting soft.

Sighing, she swung the crossbow onto her back. She yanked the ruined mess that had been the man's shirt out from under his body and tied it around his arm as tightly as she could. Rowan wasn't sure how much bleeding that would actually stop at this point, but it would be better than nothing.

Rolling him onto his back was a struggle. The werebear was *not* a small man. But Rowan wasn't a dainty woman, and she managed. When she lifted him by the armpits, his bloody arm pressed into her clothes.

You wear red for a reason, she reminded herself.

"Alright, Bear, let's hope you're not too far gone by the time Grandmother gets her hands on you."

In which there are reunions

Wynne was just finishing her second bowl of porridge when the little cottage's front door opened. Wynne looked up, expecting to see Rowan with her fierce scowl and crossbow, and was surprised by a tiny old woman with a wide, glowing smile that made her eyes crinkle at the corners. Silvery hair that must have been at least waist-length was piled and pinned atop her head. She carried a large basket over one arm and a wool shawl over the other.

"Glad to see you're awake." The woman glanced at the near-empty bowl in Wynne's lap. "And with an appetite, too. Good. I'll be with you shortly. These things won't put themselves away, you know."

She placed the basket on the table and began to unpack it, humming as she worked. A rasher of bacon, a loaf of bread, and various other pantry essentials soon covered the table's surface.

"Do you need any help?" Wynne asked,

shifting towards the edge of the bed. Only one foot made it to the floor before Rowan's grandmother pinned her in place with a fierce scowl.

"Don't you even dare think about standing up yet, young lady! Your body has been through quite enough and will thank you to remain in bed a while longer."

Sufficiently chastised, Wynne settled back against the pillows. Now that she'd eaten, her exhausted body longed to slip back into slumber and dream away the lingering effects of the siphoning sickness. She resisted the urge. Every moment she stayed too close to Green Briar was another moment Windholt's men could burst through the door. She had to get out of here as quickly as possible.

"Now then," her host said when all her purchases were properly stored, "A proper introduction is in order, I believe. You've already met my granddaughter, Rowan. Surly thing, isn't she? I am Edna."

"Goldie."

Wynne didn't like the knowing smile the old woman gave her one bit, But all Edna said was, "What an appropriate name. Let's take a look at how that cut on your foot is doing, hm?"

Wynne sat silent and motionless through the process as her foot was unwrapped, poked and prodded, and re-wrapped with fresh poultice. As badly as she wanted to continue her escape, she had to admit she wouldn't get very far with an infected cut on her foot.

"It's not infected, but you should stay off of it as much as possible for a few more days, at least. I had to put a few stitches in while you were asleep."

"A few days?" Wynne repeated. "That's impossible. I have to get out of here."

"I'm sorry, my dear, but I don't make the rules. It's Mother Nature who decrees the rate at which living things mend, not I."

"But—"

"No buts! You are going to stay here and mend for at least two days if I have to tie you to the bedpost. Do you understand?"

"But Windholt—"

"Will not find you here, dear girl. I have made sure of that." Edna's expression darkened as she spoke, a hard glint in her steely eyes. Then the expression was gone, replaced with her effervescent smile. "Give an old witch some credit, yes? Now, more sleep would be the best thing with all you've been through. Do you need some poppy to help you drift off?"

Wynne sighed, half from exasperation and half from resignation, but her eyelids were heavy. "No, I'm fine."

"Suit yourself. Just holler if you need anything. I'll just be right outside tending to the rose bushes."

Wynne had just about drifted off when a commotion outside jolted her back to wakefulness. She jerked upright, eyes wide and heart hammering. Had Windholt's lackeys found her?

A muffled voice that might have been Rowan's was speaking. Wynne couldn't make out the words, but Edna's response carried.

"Second wounded thing you've brought home in one day. You're going soft, Rowan. Bring him inside."

The door slammed open, and Rowan's back entered the cottage first, her body blocking Wynne's view. She was dragging something—presumably the him in the question—into the cottage.

"We're going to have to get him up onto the table," Edna said. She entered last, carrying the man's feet.

"He's a heavy bastard," Rowan complained. She was puffing with the effort of just moving him across the room.

"Do you need help?" Wynne asked.

"You just stay right where you are," Edna snapped. "I don't need two bleeding patients."

"On the count of three," Rowan said. "One — two— three—"

With a great heave, they hoisted the large man onto the kitchen table. From her vantage point, Wynne could see he was shirtless. He was pallid beneath his tan and blood streaked his muscled torso. When Rowan stepped away from his head, Wynne gasped.

Callum.

Wynne fell, her limbs tangling in the sheets in her rush to get to him. She scrambled across the room, half crawling, half running, oblivious to Edna's shouts and the tearing sensation in the sole of her foot.

"Callum! Callum!" She grasped his face in both hands, tears streaming freely. Her brain couldn't quite process what she was seeing. There was so much blood. "Callum, wake up! Callum!"

Strong hands grasped Wynne's upper arms, trying to pull her away from him. Wynne whirled on Rowan, landing a solid punch to the woman's face.

"What did you do to him?!" Wynne screamed.

She swung again, but this time Rowan was prepared. She blocked the blow and grabbed Wynne's wrist, pulling her into a hold that twisted her arm painfully.

"You have to calm down and let us help him or he'll die," Rowan said bluntly. "Now. Sit. Down." She released Wynne, who fell to the floor in a crumpled heap.

Callum had come after her. It was the only explanation for why he was here. She'd worried he'd be hurt by her unexplained disappearance, but she'd never imagined he'd actually come looking for her.

He knew something wasn't right. He knew I didn't leave voluntarily. That's why he came after me. And now—and now—oh, stars, this is all my fault! I should've told him not to come with me to Wickersburg. I should've made him listen. She sobbed as the condemnations rolled through her mind. Callum was going to die, and it was all her fault.

"I guess you were telling the truth, Bear," Rowan muttered. Her dark eyes turned from Wynne sobbing on the floor to the half-dead man on the table. "Now don't die on us before you get to have your happy reunion."

"We don't have time for this nonsense," Edna snapped. Her lips were set in a grim line as she studied Callum's body. "It's just a flesh wound, but something else is wrong. We need to stop the bleeding. Quickly. Wynne, come here."

Wynne scrambled to her feet and hobbled to Edna's side, ignoring the pain in her foot and the blood seeping through her bandages.

"Since you're already up, you can help. Keep this pressed tight on the wound. As tight as you can. Rowan, heat the water. Now."

It seemed to Wynne that everything was happening in slow motion. Edna barked orders and riffled through jars on shelves. Rowan did everything her grandmother asked with brisk efficiency. Only Wynne stood still, pressing the blood-soaked shirt to Callum's arm as tears streamed down her face.

"Move, I have to clean it," Edna said. She pushed Wynne out of the way with surprising gentleness.

She globbed what looked like honey into the wound with a small stick before taking the sterilized needle and thread Rowan handed her. Blood and honey slicked her fingers as she worked, snipping the thread after each tidy stitch. Her mouth moved as she made each stitch, and Wynne felt an electric crackle in the air. Edna was using magic.

"That should do it," the witch said at last. "Put the poultice on it and wrap it up, I need to wash my hands."

Rowan took over, carefully wrapping Callum's upper arm with clean bandages. When she was done, Edna placed a pile of blankets under his legs.

"His heart needs all the blood it can get," she explained. "We'll leave him on the table for now while I look at your foot. I expect you've pulled the stitches." Indeed, blood stained the floor where Wynne had stood during the surgery.

"Is he going to live?" Wynne asked, more whimper than question.

"I believe so. The fool boy was already anemic when he was shot. It looks like this isn't the first fight he's been in recently."

Rowan snorted. "It wasn't much of a fight."

"If he wasn't a werebeast, I doubt he'd be alive at all," Edna continued, as if Rowan hadn't spoken. "For now, we'll just observe and try to get some fluids in him."

When he awoke, Callum's first impression was of golden waves and firelight. It took several moments of blinking before his bleary vision resolved itself into something his brain could make sense of. He was lying in an unfamiliar bed staring at a head of blond hair that rested on his good shoulder —the one that wasn't throbbing with a deep, dull ache.

He closed his eyes. This had to be a dream brought on by fever or whatever potion his menders had poured down his throat while he was unconscious. Nevertheless, his good arm tightened about the woman, pulling her as close as the bedsheets would allow. She murmured in her sleep, one hand clutching the sheet covering his chest. He smiled into her hair, breathing deep her sweet scent.

Wynne.

He tried to say her name aloud, but his voice came out as a strangled sigh, his mouth and throat dry as bone.

Wynne stirred again, then lifted her head, blinking sleepily. He could see the moment when she came to true wakefulness. The relief and joy in her eyes hit him like a physical blow.

"You're awake," she whispered. She brushed back the stray hair that clung to his sweaty brow. "Thank all the stars in all the heavens, I was so afraid."

Callum closed his eyes, reveling in that small touch. He sighed in contentment as her delicate fingers combed through his hair. Yes, surely this was just a dream. A hallucination. When he woke, he would be alone in some strange bed or dead.

"I'm dreaming," he croaked. "One last sweet dream."

"No, you're not. I'm right here. It's going to be okay." She leaned up and pressed a kiss to his forehead. "Just rest. You have a lot of healing to do, even for a werebear. Edna says you seem to be suffering from more blood loss than what the crossbow caused."

"Werecats..." Callum trailed off, lacking the strength and alertness to explain. He was already slipping back under the black abyss of unconsciousness.

In which the villain stinks

If there was one thing Ainsley Crichton, Lord of Windholt, despised, it was being dirty. Under ordinary circumstances, he wouldn't have lowered himself to such a state as traipsing through the forest with common rabble. However, this quarry had proven particularly elusive, and he wasn't about to let these bumbling blockheads he employed lose her again. He should have had a small army with him, but Forswraithe had suddenly declined to send any of his men when the girl's whereabouts were described. Windholt's thinly veiled threats hadn't changed his decision, a fact that annoyed Windholt more than it worried him.

"You're *sure* the siphon is in this cottage?" He didn't bother to keep the contempt out of his voice.

Gil Hardy, the self-proclaimed "eldest Hardy brother," grunted in what Windholt supposed was meant to be affirmation. Gil was the taciturn sort, and he didn't change that habit just because a lord was speaking to him. Windholt vacillated between finding the trait amusing and irritating. Right now it was decidedly irritating. Everything was irritating when you were running on two hours of sleep.

"And the bear is with her?" Arlo asked, causing Windholt to roll his eyes.

"Stars and ashes, Arlo," Windholt swore. He was quickly losing his patience with this nonsense. "There's four of us and one of him. What do you really expect him to do against those odds?"

"Everyone in Snoaksly-on-Barnham knows not to mess with the Bertram brothers, sir. I don't think you should underestimate him."

"I'll rip his throat out myself," Gil growled, cracking his knuckles.

Oh, now *you want to talk,* Windholt thought acidly.

"Because that worked out so well last time," Arlo shot back.

His bravado in taunting the werecat was short-lived, however. When Gil stalked toward him, the wereweasel scuttled backward. It almost made Windholt laugh the way that Gil looked and acted exactly like every dim-witted villain in a theatre show. The Hardy triplets were all alike, meat-bags full of muscle with very little brain beyond what was required to keep them breathing. Their solution to every problem was to hit—or bite—it until it went away or died.

"What did ye say, Rat?"

Arlo gulped but straightened his spine a

little, glancing at Windholt to make sure his boss wasn't going to let the cat tear out his jugular for practice.

"I *said* that plan didn't work out so well for you last time."

"Why ye little—" Gil took a clearly telegraphed swipe at Arlo, who nimbly avoided it.

The werecat snarled as the momentum of his swing carried him past his opponent, who hooked a foot around his ankle. The takedown worked better than Arlo could have possibly hoped, and Gil went face first into the tree litter.

"Enough," Windholt barked.

Gil snarled and leapt up, prepared for another attack.

"I *said* that's *enough*," Windholt repeated. "You're wasting time and energy better saved for the bear."

Gil threw Arlo a venomous glare but didn't take another step. Windholt wasn't sure if it was the money his employment provided or revenge against the werebear that was worth more to the werecat than skinning Arlo's cowardly hide. He didn't care, so long as the blond idiot obeyed.

"This way," Gil rumbled, shoving past his antagonist. His upper lip curled as he shot Arlo a significant look. "An' keep quiet. We'll be in earshot soon." He pulled something out of a pouch on his belt. "Take this an' rub it on ye."

Windholt's nose wrinkled at the stench of the leaves Gil shoved into his hands. "What *is* this?"

"Hunter's Friend. To most people, it's just a weed, but it has one very important use: it covers up yer scent and confuses animals' senses. If ye don't use it, the bear will smell us coming from miles away. An' I mean *miles*. Them bastards have sharp noses. Crush it like this." He demonstrated, rolling a wad of leaves between his palms. "It releases the oils what makes it work." When he held out his hands for inspection, they were covered in a thin sheen of oil. The odor coming off them was positively foul.

Windholt mimicked him, struggling against his gag reflex the whole time.

"Good. Now rub it all over. 'Specially the pits." Gil proceeded to lead by example, smearing the vile plant juice all over his grimy clothes. "I've already applied some today, so I don't need much." He leaned toward Windholt, sniffing experimentally.

"I beg your pardon!"

"No offense boss, but you're going to need a lot of this to cover up that flower water ye rich people like to spray everywhere. I ain't got no bear nose and I could smell ye coming."

"And you're saying he won't smell this stench?" Windholt asked between dry heaves.

The smell was actually making his eyes water. The oils from the plant were leaving dark patches in the fabric of his clothes. He threw the last handful of repulsive leaves aside and swallowed against the vomit rising in his throat.

"It'll die down as it mixes with yer normal

smell. Ye'll become something of a background noise in the symphony of odors in the forest."

"Gil, do you even know what a symphony is?"

The werecat's self-satisfied expression faltered.

"I thought not. Let's go."

"Absolutely remarkable," Edna said, as Wynne handed her a clean roll of bandages. The elderly witch was bent over the comatose Callum, examining the half-healed wound in his arm. "Last night he seemed to be on death's door and this morning it's half-healed."

"What about the fever he had in the night?" The fever had scared Wynne. He'd been so sweaty and sticky.

"Werebeasts always think themselves immune to pesky things like germs and ill-humors. And they are remarkably resilient —" Edna slathered a thick paste onto the wound as she spoke. "But your man here has lost a lot of blood recently. You see these cuts?" She pointed to a pink line of freshly healed flesh. "His back is covered in them. He lost a lot of blood recently and even his werebeast magic can't replace it that fast. His whole body is weaker and more susceptible than usual."

"But he's going to be okay?"

"With rest and the right treatment, yes.

We got him stitched in time and I don't see any signs of putrefaction. Unfortunately, I don't have the right medicinals on hand for building up the blood. I'll have to make a trip into the forest. Help me with this, dear."

Wynne held Callum's arm aloft while Edna re-wrapped the bandages. Edna had dosed him with a sleeping draught earlier that morning when Wynne told her he'd awoken in the night, saying it was best if he just slept and let his body heal. The potion kept him out cold all through having his arm poked and prodded and cleaned with a stinging solution of alcohol.

"He'll probably wake up soon," Edna announced.

She went to the kitchen space and pulled down a mortar and pestle. She added several things from various jars and bags to it, humming while she worked. When it was all ground into a fine powder, she dumped it into one of the earthenware bowls she and Rowan ate out of.

"When he wakes up, fix him some porridge with this powder. Once it's mixed with the syrup and spices, he won't even taste it. It will help fight off any infection."

Wynne wasn't entirely convinced that Callum wouldn't taste it but she'd make him gag down a whole pitcher of whatever vile concoction Edna prescribed if it meant he'd live.

The two of them found Rowan outside. The sun was newly risen, but Rowan looked like she'd been up for hours. Her dark hair was freshly plaited, and she was wearing her signature red cloak over wool and leather forest garb. Instead of the crossbow, she carried an ordinary bow. Her arrows were fletched with goose feathers dyed crimson Wynne noted with amusement. Rowan might pretend to be all about practicality, but the woman certainly had a flair for the dramatic.

"I'm going hunting. The bear's going to need more than porridge if he's going to heal." She frowned. "Grandmother, where's your shawl? It's barely spring."

"Poppycock. I'll be fine," Edna said with a dismissive wave.

Rowan heaved a heavy sigh and stomped back into the cottage. Wynne struggled to smother a smile when she reappeared with her grandmother's thick wrap over one arm.

"I'll walk with you for a while. There are still dangerous men in the forest."

Edna rolled her eyes but didn't argue. She seemed to be scanning the edges of the forest, as if looking for something. Wynne felt a chill run up her spine. Suddenly, it felt like unseen eyes were watching her from every direction.

"Stay in the cottage and keep the curtains drawn," Edna said, her sharp gaze now locked on Wynne. "We'll be back before dark."

Wynne didn't argue and hurried inside, barring the door behind her.

In which Goldilocks thinks stupid thoughts

Morning sunlight was streaming through the cottage's windows, illuminating its cozy interior. Callum groaned and struggled to sit up. Wynne was no longer beside him and for a moment he thought perhaps it had been a dream after all. Despair was just settling in when Wynne came through the front door, blasting it away.

"It wasn't a dream," he said. His voice was hoarse, the sound of it making him wince.

"Let me get you some water. Rowan pulled some fresh from the well this morning." She limped towards a bucket hung near the fireplace.

Callum frowned at the way she was moving before he remembered the blood he'd found in the forest.

The water soothed his parched throat, and he found speaking easier. Wynne moved to refill the cup, but Callum caught her hand and tugged her back. When she took a seat on the edge of the bed, he plucked the cup from her grasp and sat it on the bedside table. He didn't let go of her hand.

"How did you escape?"

She told him of Mared and the secret passageways within Green Briar's walls. How the two of them had made it to the back of the property before Windholt caught up with her. When she showed him the burn on her wrist, Callum saw red, and he almost missed the rest of the story. She finished with meeting Rowan and waking up in the cottage much as Callum had. Except Rowan hadn't shot her, he noticed.

"I'm so glad you're alright," Wynne said. "When they dragged you in here I thought... stars above, Callum, I thought you were dead."

His lips quirked up in a small smile. "I won't pretend it wasn't close. I hadn't quite recovered from the last time somebody tried to kill me."

Wynne's brows drew together in confusion, and it was Callum's turn to tell his story. By the end of it, there were tears in Wynne's eyes and it was all Callum could do to resist pulling her close and kissing her until she forgot what had upset her in the first place.

"It's alright, sweetheart. I'm fine now." It wasn't quite the whole truth just yet. His arm would be whole in a day or so, but he'd likely need a week yet to replace all the blood he lost. It would be best to avoid any physical altercations for a while, if at all possible.

"You're *not* fine. You almost died. *Twice.*" Wynne's words were almost choked off by sobs. "Because of me."

"No, don't you do that. Don't you go taking responsibility for the actions of others." He gave in and pulled her towards him, wrapping both arms tightly around her.

For a moment he was afraid she would resist, but Wynne relaxed into the embrace. Her whole body shook with the force of her weeping. Callum just held her, stroking her hair until the worst of it subsided.

"The first time was the result of my own foolishness," he said when she was calm enough to really hear him. "And the second was because the little red hunter is a trigger-happy psycho that takes pot-shots at bears."

Wynne gave a small, hiccupping sort of laugh.

"Do you know what I really want to do right now?" he asked.

"No. What?"

"I'd really, really like to kiss you."

They eased out of their embrace enough to look at each other. Callum brushed a fresh tear from her cheek with his thumb. Even with her eyes swollen and her nose red and runny, she was still beautiful. Looking at her, staring at him with her face all tear-stained, made his heart do all sorts of unfamiliar little gymnastics inside his chest.

Is this what falling in love feels like? he wondered. Aloud, he simply said, "May I?"

She nodded, and Callum guided their lips together. The kiss started slow and tentative. After only one night of passion together, this was still barely explored territory. But before Callum knew what was happening, the urgency of it built and Wynne was suddenly in his lap. The cottage around them seemed to disappear and there was only her. The way she tasted, the way she smelled. He was utterly lost in her.

The hem of Wynne's chemise rode up around her hips and Callum couldn't help himself. His hands caressed the smooth skin of her bottom, pressing her against him. She was soft and warm, and alive. He was dizzy with the wanting of her... or maybe that was the anemia.

"Stars above, I want you so much," he whispered between kisses. "But I think I'd probably faint."

Instead, their kissing ended with the two of them cuddled on the bed, Wynne's head upon his chest. For a long time, they lay there without words, just enjoying the comfort of each other.

Callum kissed the top of her head and murmured into her hair, "Next time I want to go off on some fact-finding mission by myself, remind me that it took getting shredded by werecats and shot by a madwoman to find you again."

Wynne gave a small laugh. "Clearly, I can't leave you alone. You need adult supervision."

Callum chuckled even though he could tell her heart wasn't quite in the joke. He suspected she was still blaming herself for his injuries. There was more pain and trauma in her past than she let on. Callum hadn't forgotten how she'd insisted that coming with her would put him in unnecessary danger. From her perspective, she'd been right. The problem was that she believed *she* was the reason for the danger, not the evil intent of men like Windholt.

"Wynne?"

"Hmm?"

"I know you still think this is all your fault but don't go deciding to run off without me because you think it's for the best. If you really don't want my company, that's one thing, but don't let Windholt deprive you of... whatever this is. Okay?"

"Okay." Her answer was quiet and without much enthusiasm.

Callum tried not to sigh when she pulled away with an excuse about breakfast. Somehow in their short acquaintance they'd managed to forge a fragile trust between them. The problem now was that Wynne either didn't trust herself or didn't value herself in the way she should. Or maybe he was way off base and it was something else entirely. Whatever it was, it wasn't something he could fix for her, and he knew it. All he could do was offer her a shoulder to lean on and pray that she'd continue to accept it.

Wynne prepared Callum's breakfast, following the instructions Edna had given her earlier. She noted his grimace when he took the first bite and had to resist the urge to smirk. So much for he won't even taste it.

Despite whatever questionable flavor the medication had given the porridge, Callum ate it without protest.

"I think Rowan feels bad about shooting you," Wynne told him. "She's gone out hunting especially for you. She says you're going to need something heartier than porridge to get back on your feet again."

"How kind of her," Callum muttered.

Wynne couldn't help but laugh. Although Rowan was bristly, she seemed like a genuinely kind person at heart, though Wynne doubted Callum would see it that way for a while.

There wasn't much else to do, so she made tea. The two of them sat on the bed side by side, sipping at their cups without saying much. Wynne supposed it should be awkward, but she couldn't quite muster up the requisite discomfort. It felt good to sit with him, even in silence. To just be near him was comforting—and that was what worried her.

Eventually they'd have to talk about the future, a prospect that twisted Wynne's insides into knots. When she'd decided to sleep with him back at the inn, she'd told herself it was because she deserved a little happiness. And she'd wanted him. More than she'd ever wanted anyone or anything in her life. But now she couldn't help but wonder if it had been a mistake. How much more difficult had she made this on them by giving in to her desires? Wouldn't it have been easier to walk away if she didn't know how sweet his lips tasted?

"You didn't drug the tea, did you?" Callum's voice broke the silence and jolted her out of her negative thoughts.

"What? No, why?"

He gave her a sleepy smile. "I guess it's just my body telling me it wants more time to heal. I think I'm going to take a nap."

She took his cup and allowed herself to kiss him. It was difficult to speak around the lump forming in her throat. "I think that's a good idea."

He frowned at her, sensitive to the change in her mood. "Are you alright?"

"I'm fine. Just tired." The lie sat sour on her tongue and did nothing to ease the worry in his expression. Callum was entirely too perceptive for Wynne's peace of mind.

Don't let Windholt deprive you of whatever this is. Callum had known exactly what she was planning to do before she'd even reached the conclusion herself. But he was wrong. She couldn't ask him to face Windholt with her. Even if they came out on top, it wouldn't be the end of it. There would always be another Windholt. Another greedy soul that wanted to use her to hurt others for their own gain. This was just the latest in a long line.

Stars burn me. I'm so sorry, Callum, she thought. *I wish I could stay by your side and discover what this is, but I care about you too much already to see you get killed for my sake.*

If she were whole and hale, she could sneak away while Callum was sleeping. He would be hurt, but he would be safe. As it was, her foot needed at least a couple of days for it to heal, and it would be for the best if Edna could remove the stitches properly. By that time, Callum would probably be on the mend.

If you really don't want my company, that's one thing... Her throat tightened. Could she say the words that would make him walk away from her?

"Wynne?"

She blinked. How long had she been staring at him?

"Wynne, sweetheart. What's wrong?" He squeezed her arm gently, comfortingly. "You can talk to me. Whatever it is."

She shook her head. "It's nothing, Callum. I'm fine."

"I don't believe you, but it's okay. If you decide you want to talk about it later, I'll listen then. Alright?"

Tears beaded at the corners of her eyes despite her best efforts. "Damn it, Callum. Why do you have to be so *good*?"

He looked like he'd been poleaxed. His confused expression was so adorable that Wynne wanted to laugh and sob and kiss him all at once.

"Is that... is that a bad thing?" he asked cautiously.

"Yes! I mean, no! I mean— Just forget I said anything."

"Hmm. I'm starting to doubt the wisdom of taking a nap after all."

"No, you need to rest. I'll be here when you wake up, I promise." One tawny eyebrow lifted in challenge, and Wynne rolled her eyes. She pointed to her foot. "I'm not going anywhere fast at the moment, remember?"

Callum folded his arms, grimacing as he did so.

Wynne gave in and leaned forward to kiss him again. It was just a soft lingering of lips, nothing like the passion they'd vented earlier, but it seemed to soothe his suspicions because when they parted, she saw something else shining in his warm honey eyes. Something she didn't want to think too hard about.

Callum tensed, his eyes darting to the door behind her.

"Wha—"

He pressed a finger to her lips and shook his head slowly. His lips formed one word silently. *Company.*

In which Goldilocks finds her strength

Rowan's crossbow sat by the door, the quiver full of bolts hanging above it. Wynne dashed for the weapon. As she ripped the quiver from its peg, an axe crashed through the door. Bits of the wood went flying, forcing Wynne to cover her face. The door burst inward and Wynne stifled a gasp when Windholt strolled in behind a big blond man she'd never seen before. The stranger appeared to be unarmed, but a practical looking sword hung from Ainsley's belt.

The big man only had eyes for Callum, not even glancing around the room. Ainsley, however, turned to look at her with one of his condescending smiles. She returned it with a satisfied smirk. He didn't seem to be getting much sleep; distinct bags had formed under his eyes.

"Don't even think about laying a hand on her, Windholt." Callum's voice was low and menacing, drawing Windholt's attention away from her. Wynne quickly stashed two of the crossbow bolts in her skirt's pocket.

"Is that any way to greet company?" Windholt asked mildly. He spread his hands wide in a sort of I-mean-you-no-harm gesture.

His companion, on the other hand, growled, his fingers curling like claws. Werecat?

Where are the other two? Wynne thought. Callum had definitely mentioned three werecats.

Wynne slipped her foot onto the lathe of the crossbow, intending to cock it, but a hand grabbed her wrist. She looked up to find herself face to face with Arlo. He shook his head ever so slightly.

"You're brave to touch me," she sneered.

"Come now, lovely," Windholt said, his attention back on her. "We all know you wouldn't rip the natural gift out of a werebeast. You're far too kind for that."

Wynne cocked an eyebrow at him as she opened the channels of her gift. "Am I?"

Arlo screamed.

Wynne released his gift, allowing what she'd siphoned to flow back into his body. She'd made her point. Shaking, the wereweasel crawled away from her, clutching at his chest and sobbing. Callum and the werecat were staring at her in horror, but Windholt's expression held nothing but mild amusement.

"Don't fucking touch me." She glared down at Arlo, who was now huddled in the fetal position. "The only reason I didn't rip your miserable soul out before was because of the curse I was holding." She smirked and looked Windholt dead in the eyes. "How are you enjoying that, by the way? Sucks, doesn't it?"

Her lips trembled with the effort of keeping the smirk in place. Inside, she was screaming. Bile rose in her throat, but this was no time to vomit. She needed these werebeasts to believe she would gladly incapacitate and kill them if they pushed her.

Stars, I never wanted Callum to see me do something like this. Wynne couldn't look at him. She didn't want to see fear in his eyes. How could he ever hold her hand again after this?

"Yes, very amusing. You do have spunk." Ainsley snatched the crossbow from her with one hand and grabbed a fistful of her hair with the other. He kicked the quiver of bolts aside, setting them clattering about on the floor. Wynne could hear Callum protesting, but Ainsley blocked her view of him. "Your little tricks won't work on me, lovely."

Want to bet? she thought.

Wynne gripped his wrist like she was going to try to pull his hand out of her hair, initiating the contact she needed. She opened herself to her gift again, and the world narrowed to just her and her attacker.

Ropes of colored smoke writhed around each other like snakes inside of Windholt. The familiar taint of Callum's curse was among them, pulsing as thick and black as ever. Wynne didn't have time to pick a specific gift to siphon and she couldn't risk

Windholt using any of his stolen abilities against Callum. She gathered everything she could with her power—except the curse—and yanked.

A flood of disparate magics surged out of her victim, overwhelming her senses. She couldn't breathe, couldn't think. There was only the pull and burn of the magic as it rushed to fill every void in her soul. She didn't let go, couldn't let go. The levies that held the power back and protected her burst open and it spilled over into her physical form. Every muscle in her body seized as the magic seared through her.

Wynne's throat-rending scream drove all sane thought from Callum's mind. He lunged at the werecat, shifting in midair. The other werebeast shifted just before they collided, and the two of them went down in a tangle of fur and claws. Callum's jaws closed over the puma's neck, and he jerked his head till he heard something snap. He looked up just in time to see another cat come barreling through the door, snarling and snapping.

Callum's forepaw connected with his new opponent's face, scoring deep gouges. The cat yelped and shifted back to a man. The feline mewling became human sobbing, as the remaining Hardy brother pressed a hand to the bleeding mess that used to be his left eye.

Wynne stopped screaming and crumpled to the floor, pulling an insensate Windholt with her. Callum shifted and scrambled to her, fighting off a wave of dizziness. He ripped Windholt away from her, flinging the man like a rag doll.

"Wynne! Wynne!" She wasn't moving. Callum put his ear to her chest. Her heart was beating, but it was sluggish. "Stars, Wynne." He cradled her face in his hands, pressing his forehead to hers. "Wake up. Please wake up. What did you do, Wynne? Wynne!"

"I'm going to kill that bitch." Windholt groaned, using the far end of the table to pull himself upright. "What the *fuck* did she do?"

"Boss, he killed Gil," the werecat whimpered.

Windholt's eyes darted briefly to the dead cat. Callum thought he saw the barest hint of a shrug. The brothers were just pawns, nothing more.

"I told you not to touch her. None of you listened." Callum stood to meet Windholt's challenge. His brow was slick with cold sweat and his legs shook with the effort. He was still anemic, and his body hadn't responded well to the stress of shifting. Pain radiated from the wound in his arm and the deepest of the gashes in his back. Blood from new injuries rolled down his arms in tiny rivulets.

"Look at you," Ainsley sneered. "You can barely stand. You think you're going to fight all three of us?"

"Two," Arlo corrected. He was still curled

up on the floor where Wynne had left him after her demonstration. He pushed himself up into a sitting position, glaring at Ainsley. "Fuck that and fuck you, Crichton. Stars burn your eyes to ash; I'm done with this shit."

As Arlo spoke, Callum eased himself along the end of the table, putting it between him and Ainsley. If he could get to the fire poker, he would have something to defend himself with. The movement brought Ainsley's gaze snapping back to Callum, his hand reaching for his sword.

Callum shoved the table forward with every ounce of strength he still possessed. It was the right height to catch the shorter Windholt in the hips and the surprise of it knocked him off balance. It was the opening Callum needed to grab the poker hanging from its peg by the mantle. He brought it up like a sword. Callum had no sword training, and the poker was a makeshift weapon at best, but it *was* a weapon, and it would help keep distance between him and Windholt's blade. He sidled back towards Wynne, placing himself between her and the recovered Windholt.

Now would be a really good time to show up and start shooting things, Rowan, he thought.

"You're clever, I'll give you that," Ainsley said as he advanced. "I can see why Goldie— or what was it you called her? Wynne—likes you. She's going to be so disappointed when she wakes up and discovers your corpse."

Movement caught Callum's eye, and he

spared a glance for the werecat who was now desperately trying to stop the bleeding of his mangled eye with the sheets from the bed.

It was a mistake.

The sword came for his head, and Callum barely had time to get the poker up to block it. The shock of metal clashing against metal almost made him drop it.

Windholt laughed and stepped back lightly, disengaging. "You have no idea what you're doing, do you? This has all been dumb animal luck so far."

Callum gritted his teeth. He wouldn't give Windholt the satisfaction of an answer; they both knew he was right. Callum's arms felt like lead. He was barely keeping the fire poker aloft. Another strike from Windholt like that would go right through his flimsy defense.

Windholt came at him again. Callum managed to keep the sharp edge of the sword from his face, but this time Windholt pressed in, forcing Callum backward. He nearly tripped over Wynne and soon found himself backed against the window. The crossed blade and poker were inches from his nose with Windholt angling to get a cut at his neck. A confident smirk twisted Windholt's lips and Callum knew the man was just toying with him.

Blood erupted from Windholt's mouth, splattering Callum's face and torso. A crossbow bolt protruded from the side of his neck. Confusion filled Windholt's expression as he stumbled back, one hand coming up to touch the projectile lodged in his throat.

Panic replaced confusion as more blood frothed over his lips. He dropped the sword to claw at the bolt with both hands. Wynne stood behind him, her hand smeared with blood.

There was the distinct sound of another sword being unsheathed. Before Callum could comprehend what was happening, Arlo had driven his blade through Ainsley's heart.

"I should have done that a long time ago," the wereweasel said. He wiped his blade on his former employer's shirt.

"Coward," the werecat snarled.

"Oh, shut up, Elliot. I didn't see you getting involved again." He turned his attention to Callum and Wynne. "I don't want any quarrel with you. Don't give me any grief and I'll tell the blockheads back at Green Briar you're all dead. Not that any of them are likely to want to avenge this sack of shit's death, anyway." He kicked Windholt's corpse for emphasis.

"Why?" Wynne asked. Her voice was soft and broken. From the way her hands were shaking, Callum thought she might be going into shock.

"Like I said, I'm done. I don't want anything more to do with this nonsense. I'm going back to Green Briar, loading my pockets up with this fool's money, and heading off to make a new start somewhere that's never heard of Lord Windholt. Now, are you going to make this difficult and die pointlessly, or are you going to let me go on my way?"

Callum felt his lip curl in spite of himself. "Awful big talk for a wereweasel."

Arlo rolled his eyes. "You're about two seconds away from collapsing whether I cut your head off or not. Stars, you big predators are all arrogant bastards."

"What about him?" Callum gestured at Elliot, who was still snarling and pressing Rowan's bedsheets to his eye-socket.

"Kill him. Let him go. I don't give a fuck."

In a blink, Arlo was gone, replaced by the largest weasel Callum had ever seen. It gave them a sort of salute with its furry little paw, then darted out the open door.

Wynne started to follow, but Callum reached out and caught her wrist. "Let him go. We'd never catch him anyway. And we have bigger problems to deal with."

He released her and picked up the discarded crossbow. This was a weapon he *did* know how to use. He set the string and plucked one of the bolts from the floor and placed it on the groove.

"Let's go," Callum said, pointing the weapon at the werecat. He nodded towards Windholt's body. "Pick him up."

"You going to shoot me?"

"Not unless you give me a reason to. Now move."

When the corpse was a good distance away, Callum forced Elliot back into the cottage, keeping the crossbow pointed at his head while Wynne tied his wrists and ankles with a length of rope from one of their packs. It took longer than it should have because her hands were trembling violently.

Finally, Callum backed away, drawing Wynne with him. "Are you alright?" he asked, keeping his tone low to give Wynne the illusion of privacy. He knew the werecat would be able to hear everything they said anyway, but she didn't need to know that.

"I just killed a man," she whispered. Tears were forming in her eyes and the trembling had spread to the rest of her body. There was still blood, now cool and tacky, on her right hand. She wiped at it with her left, doing more to smear it than remove it. "Stars, Callum, I *killed* him."

"Technically Arlo killed him."

"He would have died anyway."

"You did what you had to do, Wynne." He wanted to hug her, but he was bloody and sweaty and about to fall over.

She wasn't looking at him. Her eyes were trained on the puddle of blood in the middle of the cottage floor.

He put his body between her and it. "Come on, let's get you cleaned up."

The adrenaline that allowed her to stab Windholt and keep moving in the wake of his death was wearing off, and Wynne felt herself slipping. Numbness was being replaced by a burning pain unlike anything she'd ever experienced. Usually siphoning sickness left her feeling burned just beneath the skin along the channels of her gift, but this was different. The sensation was everywhere, driving deep into her muscles. And it was growing.

What have I done?

Every siphon knew they could only siphon one magic at a time. If they weren't taught this basic rule, they learned it the hard way, eventually. There was a limit to what their souls could hold, and it was impossible to stretch beyond that limit.

Except she had.

Wynne had grabbed every stolen gift inside Ainsley's body—she didn't even know how many—and siphoned them in one explosive draw. It should have been impossible. It *was* impossible. Or so they had thought.

She sat on the kitchen bench next to Callum and closed her eyes, trying to open herself up to her gift to examine the damage that had been done. But she couldn't find it. That empty space inside her that had existed for as long as she could recall—was gone. In its place was something warm and pulsing.

Wynne tried to touch it.

Searing pain lit up every one of her nerve endings, and Wynne shrieked before her jaw locked up. White heat erased her vision, and she was only vaguely aware of Callum grasping her arms before she slid off the bench. The two of them sank to the ground together. Wynne wanted to tell him that it hurt, that his hands on her felt like hot pokers, but she couldn't make her mouth work.

It was a relief when unconsciousness came.

In which things change

Callum barely stopped himself from shooting Rowan when she walked in the door.

"Stars and ashes," Rowan swore. "Put that thing down before you hurt someone!" She stopped to look around the cottage. "Oh, I guess it's too late for that. I knew I should have stayed here."

Callum grunted his agreement.

Rowan eyed him up and down. "You seem to have done your best to undo all my grandmother's hard work. I'm surprised you're even upright. Where's Goldie?"

"On the bed. I managed to move her there after she collapsed. Something—something happened. I think she hurt herself with her gift."

"She wouldn't tell me about her powers. Grandmother seemed to have an idea, but she wouldn't say anything either." Rowan's mouth compressed into a thin line. Clearly, she didn't appreciate being the only one in the dark.

It was Wynne's secret to share though, and he wasn't about to divulge it unless it was absolutely necessary. Given that she was now breathing normally and appeared to be resting comfortably, he didn't think that applied.

"Is all of this blood his?" Rowan hitched a thumb in Elliot's direction.

"No. Most of it belongs to Windholt and his other lackey. The bodies are out back."

Rowan's dark brows arched in surprise. "I'll get the shovel. You just rest and keep an eye on him." Her thumb jerked at the werecat. "If he so much as twitches wrong, shoot him."

Rowan came back some time later covered in mud. She barely glanced at the captive werecat at first, instead focusing on plucking the fat partridge she'd brought home with her. She had a delicious smelling stew simmering before sparing any attention for Elliot. She gave the bound werecat's wounds cursory medical attention. When he tried to bite her, she cuffed him upside the head and threatened to add to his injuries if he thought to try that again.

After that, Rowan worked with brisk efficiency tidying the cottage. Soon only Elliot's presence and the dark stains on the floor remained to tell the story. In all that time, Wynne did not wake, and Callum's fears grew. He was relieved when the witch finally walked through the door, a heavy basket overflowing with green things dangling from her arm.

He didn't know what he had expected, but

Callum found it hard to believe that this tiny woman was in any way related to the bloodthirsty Rowan. She smiled at him warmly, like he was a favored grandson come to visit after staying away too long.

"Glad to finally make your acquaintance properly, Callum," she said, placing the basket on the table before the fire. Her sharp, dark eyes took in the scene before returning to his face. "It seems you've made quite the mess while I was gone."

Callum told her all that had happened while she cleaned and salved his new cuts. The old witch tsked and sighed throughout.

"You're lucky to be breathing," Edna announced at the end of his tale. She shoved a foul-smelling concoction in his hands. "Drink this. It'll help fortify your blood and restore some of the strength you've lost."

He took a tentative sip and nearly gagged. Izzy's potions hadn't been tasty by any means, but this brew made them delicious by comparison.

"Do you know what's wrong with Wynne?" he asked.

He'd done his best to describe what Wynne had done, but in truth, all he really saw was her grab Ainsley and then start screaming. Then later, she just sort of stared off into space before letting out a shrill yelp and turning stiff as a board.

Edna shook her head. "She seems physically unharmed. The stitches in her foot even survived the altercation. The best thing for her now is probably rest, which is exactly what you should be doing. Rowan and I will take turns watching over our... guest. You sleep."

The fever started later that night. Callum awoke feeling like he was sharing the bed with a pile of hot coals. He screamed for Edna, and they did everything they could to lower her temperature.

"Is it siphoning sickness?" Callum demanded. He was pacing in the storage area away from the table and the fireplace, as out of the way as he could be in the small space. "She didn't get this hot before."

Rowan, who had been helping her grandmother by changing out cool compresses, recoiled as if she'd be slapped. "Siphoning sickness?" she repeated, whirling to glare at him. "She's a stars-burned *siphon,* and you didn't tell us? Do you realize she could kill any one of us with a single touch?"

"She could," Callum agreed. "But she wouldn't."

Edna ended the argument before it could escalate by sending Rowan out to the well for more water. Then she skimmed her hands over Wynne's upper body, her eyes shut and her lips moving silently. Callum waited with bated breath until the witch sagged back on her stool.

"If it's siphoning sickness, it's like nothing I've ever seen," Edna admitted. "When she first came here, I could feel it when I healed her. She was burned out and hollow. But this?" She shook her head. "She most certainly siphoned something but..."

"But what?" Callum demanded when her words trailed off.

"It isn't where it should be." Edna straightened up and started the scanning process over again. "Yes, it's different. Before there was a well, a vacuole inside her. But this power she's absorbed—it's taken over her entire body."

"What are you saying? What does that mean?"

"I don't know what I'm saying," Edna snapped. "I've never seen anything like this in my life. My very, very *long* life, I might add. But your friend doesn't appear to be a siphon anymore."

"That's not possible," Rowan argued. She set the bucket of water on the table with a little more force than was necessary. Her whole body radiated tension as she snatched up a cloth and began wiping up what she'd spilled.

"Rowan, my dear, you are far too young to be proclaiming what is and is not possible," Edna said with a heavy sigh. She rose and stretched. The creaks and cracks of her joints made Callum wince. "There isn't much more I can do for Wynne tonight. I'm taking these old bones to bed."

Rowan plucked a glass jar from one of the shelves before heading towards the door. "I'm giving our other *guest* another dose of sleeping draught, just to be safe. I don't need a werecat tearing my throat out in my sleep."

Within minutes the cottage was quiet

again. Callum sat on the stool by Wynne's bedside, one of her small hands wrapped in both of his. She still felt warmer to the touch than she ought to, but if Edna thought she was out of danger, then Callum would just have to trust the old healer's judgement. He settled in for a long night of watching and waiting.

The days that followed were a period of recovery. Arlo seemed to be as good as his word; no one else had come looking for them. As for Elliot, the group had to put his fate to a vote.

"We should kill him," Rowan said flatly. "He'll run off back to the village and squeal like a pig. All of Forswraithe's men will be on us before sunset."

Callum shook his head. "I don't kill people in cold blood, contrary to what some might believe." He hooked a thumb over his shoulder in the werecat's direction. "His brothers are dead because they came at me with murderous intent. That's it."

"Forswraithe won't bring his men out here anyway," Edna said, folding her arms. "Windholt was foolish and greedy; that's why he was here on his own with just a handful of his personal lackeys. None of Forswraithe's men would have dared accompany him."

Callum eyed Edna suspiciously. He was beginning to suspect that her relationship with the baron was long and complicated. He was also beginning to wonder just how powerful the elderly witch really was.

In the end, only Rowan was in favor of a summary execution. She walked out of the cottage in a huff before Callum cut the werecat's bonds.

"Go home," Callum told the werecat.

Tears formed in the big blond man's remaining eye. "What about Gil?"

Callum surprised himself when he answered. "If you want to take him back to Wickersburg, I'll help you dig him up." He paused, shifting uncomfortably. He grimaced as he spoke again, his mind conjuring up an image of Brodie and Alasdair. "For what it's worth, I'm sorry about your brothers. I know in your shoes I'd probably be wanting revenge, too."

Elliot wiped at his face, clearly trying to hide the tears. "I can't afford no proper burial anyway."

Edna checked the bandages over his eye once more and gave him a bundle of bread and hard cheese wrapped in a handkerchief. It wasn't much, but it was probably more kindness than the man deserved. Callum watched from the door until Elliot had disappeared from sight. He prayed this mercy wouldn't come back to haunt him.

Wynne slept for almost a week. Edna and Rowan tended her carefully, leaving little for

Callum to do except lie next to her and let his own wounds heal. The women made Wynne swallow water and broth and bathed her after she broke out in horrible sweats. Callum often found himself booted from the cottage during these events.

On the sixth day, Wynne opened her eyes and announced that she was hungry. Callum couldn't stop the tears of joy and relief that sprang to his eyes. Despite Edna's assurances, he'd begun to fear Wynne would simply drift away to a place he couldn't follow. Each day she'd remained comatose the fear had grown.

"Help her sit up," Edna demanded. "I'll make something suitable."

Callum slipped an arm under Wynne's shoulders. Inwardly, he cursed how frail she felt. But he sat her up and placed a kiss on top of her head before Edna elbowed him aside.

While Wynne drank the thin broth, Edna set about mixing up something else. Probably a potion, judging from the odor filling Callum's nose. Every time Edna mixed up something magical Callum wound up with stinging sinuses and watery eyes.

"Make sure she drinks this," Edna said, plopping a clay mug down on the bedside table. "I'm going out to the garden for more supplies."

And with that, the two of them were alone.

"Stars, Wynne, I thought you might not come back this time," Callum said, pressing a kiss to the back of her clammy hand. A lump had formed in his throat.

"I wasn't so sure myself," she admitted.

"Sometimes it was like a part of me was awake and aware, but I couldn't make my body move or react to anything around me. Other times I think I was dreaming."

Callum collected the empty bowl and handed her the mug. Apparently, it wasn't just his sensitive nose that objected, because Wynne's wrinkled when she lifted the concoction to her lips.

"Do I really have to drink this?"

Callum leaned in until his nose just about touched hers, ignoring the noxious fumes that made his eyes water. "I have drunk every foul thing Edna has poured down my throat this past week without complaint so I could be fit and healthy when you woke up. So, I will sing like a damn canary when she asks me whether or not you drank that." He raised his lips to press a kiss to her forehead. "Drink up."

In which Goldilocks makes a decision

The sun wasn't up yet, but Wynne was wide awake. Beside her, Callum was taking the deep, even breaths of sleep. He slept so peacefully now without the curse. Edna was another story. Wynne could hear her tossing and turning, mumbling in her sleep on a cot by the fire. Every little noise grated on Wynne's frayed nerves.

She slipped from the bed, careful not to wake Callum. Instantly, she missed the comforting warmth of his body. For a moment, she considered snuggling back under the covers and trying once more to find rest. But only for a moment.

Wynne debated whether to take her pack or not. It wasn't really hers, after all. The loss of her own belongings was irrevocable though, and she knew it would be a while before she could afford so much as a single stocking. So, she shouldered the bag, praying Callum wouldn't begrudge her for it too much. It probably wouldn't even cross his mind. He'd be upset about her leaving, but being the kindhearted soul he was, Wynne suspected he'd want her to have whatever supplies she needed.

A pang of regret stung her. She didn't want to hurt Callum by leaving without a word, but trying to say it to his face, with those honey eyes misty and pleading—no. She was far too much of a coward for that. She glanced around the darkened cottage, but there was nothing obvious she could use to write a note and she didn't dare rummage. Her handwriting was rubbish anyway; she doubted anything she did write would be legible.

I'm so sorry, Callum, she thought, staring down at him. She considered giving him a final kiss goodbye, but that might break her fragile resolve.

She slunk from the cottage on cat's paws, shutting the door behind her as softly as possible. Her foot still hurt, and she limped a bit as she started toward the forest's edge.

"And where do you think you're sneaking off to?"

Wynne winced. She'd forgotten about Rowan sleeping outside. The other woman was lying on her side on a bedroll meant for camping, propped up on one elbow.

"Well?" Rowan prompted when Wynne wasn't immediately forthcoming.

"I have to go, Rowan. You and your grandmother have been more than kind. There's no way I could ever repay your generosity. But I can't stay here. Danger follows me wherever I go, and the two of you have risked more than enough for my sake already."

Rowan snorted. "Leaving without a word in the dead of night is one hell of a way to show your appreciation, Wynne." She shifted, sitting up. "Forget about us. What about Bear Boy?"

Wynne swallowed. Her mouth suddenly felt incredibly dry.

"I know you care about him," Rowan pressed. "You lost your damn mind when you thought he was dying. Don't even try to deny it."

"I— I just can't tell him goodbye. I can't, Rowan."

It was too dark to see Rowan's expression clearly, but Wynne could practically feel the heat of the other woman's glower.

"Do you have any idea how highly that man thinks of you?" Rowan said, her voice suddenly harsh. "Stars alone know why, but he thinks you're the bravest woman to walk the face of the earth." This was punctuated by another snort. "I don't know where he gets that from, because all I see is cowardice."

"That's not fair, Rowan. You don't know anything about me."

"I know you're running away."

"I'm *protecting* him." Wynne had to grind the words out.

"Protecting him from what exactly? You can't even siphon anymore, can you? It's not like you're going to suck his soul out in his sleep."

"I would *never* do that to him." It was all

Wynne could do not to shout. Rowan's insinuation that she had no control over her gift infuriated her. And to even *suggest* that she might do such a thing to him on purpose...

"Then what? Windholt is dead."

"Forswraithe isn't. Arlo isn't. That werecat, whatever his name is, isn't."

Rowan folded her arms and leaned back against the cottage's wall. "The werecat's grudge is with Callum anyway; don't get sidetracked. You're not afraid of some faceless villain, you're afraid of getting hurt."

"That's not—"

"You're afraid that you'll get attached and then another man like Windholt will show up and Callum will decide you're not worth the effort to protect."

Wynne shook her head. "No. I'm afraid that another will come, and another, and another until one of them finally manages to take me or kill Callum. I couldn't live with myself if I knew Callum was hurt or dead because of me. Stars, Rowan, he's *already* been hurt because of me."

"So, you're going to hurt him more by running away in the middle of the night?"

"It's almost dawn," Wynne protested, and she was glad she couldn't see the glare Rowan was giving her.

"Semantics. You're running away because you're too much of a coward to let anyone in. But you *want* to let him in, and you're afraid he'll convince you to stay if you give him a chance to plead his case."

Tears pricked Wynne's eyes. Whether they

were from anger at Rowan or herself, she wasn't sure. *He already did plead his case,* she thought. *If you really don't want my company, that's one thing…*

"You're right about one thing, Rowan. I *am* too much of a coward to say the words that would make Callum leave. I *can't* tell him that I don't want his company. That I don't want *him.* Because I *do.* But I can't have him. That's not my lot in life."

"You really are an idiot," Rowan grumbled. "You're not leaving tonight if I have to knock you out and drag you back inside myself. It's not safe. So go back in there, crawl back into bed, and think again on whether or not you really want to do this. When it's light out, if you still want to go, Grandmother and I will help you. But you don't get to wander off in the dark and get yourself killed after all that effort we put in to keep you alive. Got it?"

What wind was left in Wynne's sails abandoned her. Rowan was right. It was the height of folly to run off into unfamiliar woods in the dark. Especially when Forswraithe's men might still be looking for her. "Fine," she snapped. "I'll go back to bed. But I'm holding you to your word."

Wynne crept back into the cottage. It was still quiet, aside from Edna's mumbling and Callum's soft breathing. With a sigh, Wynne slipped the pack from her shoulder and set it gently back where she'd found it. When she crawled back into bed, Callum rolled over, one arm wrapping over her waist.

"Where'd you go?" The question was a sleepy mumble.

"I had to pee," she whispered. "Go back to sleep."

"I heard voices."

Wynne groaned inwardly. Of course, he had. She and Rowan hadn't exactly been quiet, and his hearing was better than average. "I woke Rowan by mistake. It was nothing."

"You're a terrible liar, Wynne." But he nuzzled her shoulder as he said it. His voice was warm and heavy with sleep and the sound of it made tears burn her eyes again.

A hard lump formed in her throat that made it hard to breathe. She swallowed, trying to fight back the sobs that would give her away. "Just go back to sleep," she whispered, pressing first a kiss and then her cheek to his forehead.

He sighed with contentment and his breathing deepened.

She thought sleep would be impossible, but with Callum's warmth pressed against her side she found her eyelids growing heavier.

If you really don't want my company, that's one thing...

Stars, she thought. *There's nothing I want more.*

"Hmm," Edna said for the tenth time in as many minutes.

"What?" Wynne and Rowan asked in unison.

Wynne had grown more nervous with every second that Edna's hands grazed over her body. After breakfast, Edna had announced it was time for another check-up and Callum had made himself scarce. Now it was just the three of them while Edna worked whatever magic it was that let her examine Wynne's gift.

"It seems your body is finally integrating with the different magics you siphoned. I think that fever was your body going through a rejection phase, burning off what it couldn't assimilate," the old witch explained. "I wouldn't try accessing the magic just yet, but in a few days, I'd say you'll be able to do all sorts of interesting things that you couldn't before."

"What are you talking about?" Wynne squeaked. It was one thing to think she'd burnt out her gift for good, and another entirely to think she'd gained a new one. "Siphons don't assimilate the magic they take from others. We're just—" she struggled to find the right word, "—temporary vessels."

"What happens when a siphon tries to take too much magic at once?" Edna asked, her tone far too knowing for Wynne's liking.

"It makes us sick. Although, some siphons claim to have more... er, capacity than others. I'd never really pushed the boundaries of my gift." She met Rowan's disapproving glare with one of her own. "I didn't like using it."

Edna nodded. "It seems you blew way past the boundaries of your gift and sort of, well, burst that vacuole inside you that stored the magic. With nowhere else to go, it flooded the rest of your body and soul, much like it would another person."

"You mean I actually stole Ainsley's stolen gifts for myself?"

"Shouldn't that have killed her?" Rowan cut in. "No offense," she added, glancing at Wynne's scowl.

"In theory, yes," Edna said. "And had she not been here when it happened, it probably would have. Had we not managed that fever, it likely would have consumed her." She turned her attention back to Wynne. "Despite what I told your young man, it's something of a miracle you survived. What were you thinking, trying to siphon that much at once?"

"I wasn't really thinking at all," Wynne admitted. "I just knew I couldn't let that man use his stolen gifts on Callum."

"Will she ever be able to siphon again?" Rowan asked. She stood with her arms folded and a frown pulling at her lips.

"I don't know," Edna admitted. "Maybe her gift will heal itself. Maybe it won't. Only time will tell. It would probably be best if you stayed with us a while longer until we can be certain of what the magic has done to you. I believe you to be through the worst of it but—"

"I can't," Wynne said, interrupting whatever scary thought Edna was about to put in her head. "I've already put you and Rowan in far too much danger as it is. I need to get away from here before Forswraithe decides to come looking for his friend."

Rowan snorted a laugh. "That's not likely to happen. Whatever Windholt held over Forswraithe's head died with him. I expect they're having a party at Green Briar right about now."

Wynne's brow furrowed. "I don't understand."

"Don't worry about it, child." Edna patted her knee. "The local politics around here are a mess, but not something you need to worry about."

"Look at it this way," Rowan said, "if you learn to use whatever new magic you have at your disposal, no one will ever think you could be a siphon, even if your ability does heal itself. And if Windholt wanted those abilities for himself, there's bound to be something useful for self-defense mixed up in there."

Something that felt dangerously like hope blossomed in Wynne's chest. If she could defend herself, she wouldn't have to run anymore. Hesitantly, she tried to reach that place deep inside her where her gift used to be. Several different threads of magic leapt at her touch. She plucked at one, and instantly her palms felt warm. Wynne lifted one hand and a flame burst to life above her palm. Rowan yelped and leapt back, but Edna just chuckled.

"Why don't we go out back and see what you can do, hm?" the old witch suggested. "Somehow I have a feeling we're going to want a lot of space for these experiments."

Breakfast had been a quiet affair in which everyone had avoided the topic of Wynne's pre-dawn misadventure. Callum tried to catch her eye and engage her in conversation, but all his attempts had fallen flat.

The women spent a lot of time in quiet discussions after the meal. Callum had eventually taken the hint—Rowan's blatantly hostile stares—and made himself scarce while they discussed whatever it was that magically inclined women discussed. When he finally wandered back into the cottage that evening, they seem to have reached a consensus, because the atmosphere was markedly different. And Wynne was smiling.

"Callum, can we take a walk?" Wynne asked after dinner.

He glanced at Edna, who made shooing motions with a conspiratorial grin.

Spring was well and truly with them now, and the night wasn't as chilly as Callum had expected. The sky was cloudless, giving them a full view of the waning moon and a vast array of shining stars.

"I think it's time we give Edna and Rowan back their bed, don't you?"

Callum tensed. Before the incident with Windholt, Wynne had been on the brink of leaving him behind. He was worried the encounter had done nothing to change her mind, and this morning had strongly reinforced that impression. Now he braced himself for what was to come next. Stars above, when did it become so hard to think about her leaving him? *Why* was it so hard?

"Do you—" She paused. "Do you think we could convince the people of Snoaksly-on-Barnham that I'm not a thief?"

It took a few seconds for the meaning of her question to penetrate. Callum stopped walking and whirled Wynne around gently so they stood face to face in the moonlight.

"I think they could be persuaded," he said, almost hesitantly. His heart was doing a funny double-time. Did he dare to hope? "W-why do you ask?"

"Callum, I've been running all my life and I'm tired of it. There's nothing in this world I'd like more than to have a place of my own to call home."

"You could make your home anywhere. You don't need to convince Snoaksly-on-Barnham of your innocence."

"You're right. I could make my home anywhere. But..." She bit her lip. "I'd really like to make it somewhere close to yours."

There was a long moment of silence in which Wynne stared at him with a mix of fear and hope in her eyes. Callum stared back at her dumbly, his brain trying to form a coherent sentence. What it came up with was, "Could it be you like me just a wee bit, Goldie?"

Wynne rolled her eyes, and he grinned at her. Then her expression turned serious. "If you keep calling me that, I'm going to start calling you Baby Bear."

"And I'll pummel Brodie thrice for each time that you do," he vowed.

They shared a good laugh before Wynne stepped in and wrapped her arms around his middle. Callum returned the embrace, holding her tight and burying his nose in her hair.

"Did you mean what you said back in Wickersburg?" Wynne asked, the question slightly muffled by his shirt.

He chuckled. "I said a lot of things in Wickersburg, Wynne. I'm afraid you'll have to forgive me and be more specific."

"The part about feeling... things."

"Ah." Callum broke their embrace, holding her out at arm's length so she could see his expression. He wanted her to see his sincerity as much as hear it. "I meant every word. There is nothing I want more than the opportunity to get to know you properly. To —" He searched for the right word— "court you the way a woman deserves to be courted."

"You mean like going for walks and picnics?" Her eyes lit up and Callum remembered their little moment in the meadow.

He couldn't help it—his grin turned sly. "Like picnics in empty meadows with no witness but the sun in the sky," he confirmed.

"I'd like that," she whispered, leaning towards him with her face upturned.

Callum took it as an invitation and brought his mouth down on hers gently. Too gently, apparently, because Wynne nipped his lower lip and pulled back with a sly grin of her own. "What about no witnesses but the stars?"

In which Goldilocks finds a home that is "just right"

I f you can't keep your eyes closed, I'm going to have to blindfold you."

Wynne laughed at Callum's good-natured threat but gamely put her hands over her eyes, allowing him to guide her with one big, warm palm on the small of her back. She didn't know why he was being so secretive. She'd been to the site many times while it was under construction and involved in every step of the planning.

"You have to cover your eyes to get the full effect," he said. "Careful, don't trip."

"Callum, how long do I have to keep this up for? My arms are getting tired."

"Almost there—and—now!" He pried her hands away dramatically, revealing the little cottage on the edge of the woods that he, his brothers, and Bleddyn had spent the last three months constructing.

Wynne gasped. She had thought she knew what to expect, but Callum was right. It was everything she'd asked for and so much more. In the week since she'd last been to the build site, every little "wouldn't it be nice" detail she'd ever mentioned in passing had materialized. Where a plain little cabin had once sat was a cozy little fairytale cottage. White daisies filled boxes under the windows, the shutters of which had been whitewashed. Rose bushes—where had he found mature bushes?—flanked the doorway. A decorative path of steppingstones meandered its way through a dooryard overgrown with thick grasses and wildflowers.

"It's beautiful," she whispered.

"You really like it?" Callum's expression was anxious. "I thought you might be upset that I planted the garden without you, but I really wanted it to be a surprise."

"It's prefect," she assured him, standing on tiptoe to kiss his cheek.

He grinned. "Then you're going to love the inside. Come on!"

The interior was as finished as the exterior, and Wynne found herself blinking back tears. She ran her hand over the top of the new iron wood stove that dominated the little kitchen area. Frilly white curtains framed a window that looked out over an herb garden to the side of the house; Callum had promised to teach her how to cook, something she'd never had the chance to learn before.

Two doors led off the main room. One in the kitchen area opened into a pantry, which then led out to the herb garden. The other door was hung with curtains dyed a pale green. Wynne knew from the plans that it led to her very own bedroom.

"I still can't believe you really built me a house." She touched the crisp linen of her new tablecloth as she spoke. Someone—probably Callum—had placed a vase full of summer wildflowers in the center of the table, a riot of colors that popped against the white fabric.

"You said you wanted a home of your own."

"I know. I just can't believe that it exists." Wynne twirled in the space.

It wasn't much bigger than Edna and Rowan's tiny cottage, but it seemed like a mansion to her. She'd never had a place she could truly call her own before.

"And it's all yours," Callum said. "No one will ever take it away from you. You're close enough to the village to be safe, but far enough away to have your privacy. And far enough away from a certain werewolf that the full moon shouldn't be a problem."

"It won't be a problem," she said, wrapping her arms around his neck and pulling his head down so their noses touched. "You know why?"

"Why?" His eyes twinkled. He didn't mind playing her game one bit.

"Because you'll be here on those nights to protect me. Won't you?"

"Of course, sweetheart." He gave her lips a quick peck. "Full moon nights." Another peck. "New moon nights." And another. "Any night you want me, I'll be right here."

"You sure your brothers won't mind you being gone so much?"

Callum smirked. "They'll live."

"Is there a bed in that back bedroom we haven't explored yet?"

Callum's eyes took on a hungry gleam that made her toes curl in the best way. "I believe there is."

"And there's plenty of light."

"It's the middle of the afternoon," he agreed.

"Well then, Mister Bear, I believe we have a problem."

She shrieked with laughter when he scooped her up, his long legs devouring the distance to the bedroom. He charged through the curtains and tossed her onto a tall, wide bed. Wynne bounced in place, testing the latticed ropes that suspended the mattress above the ground.

"What are you doing?" Callum asked as he crawled onto the bed with her. He pinned her gently, bringing her bouncing to a halt.

"Testing the bed."

He raised one eyebrow. "Do you think Alasdair and I build inferior furniture?"

She kissed him, nibbling at his lower lip with her teeth. "Let's find out."

Later, after the sun had set and the two of them had enjoyed dinner and another round of bed testing, they lay wrapped in each other's arms. Callum was snoring softly. His brothers were expecting him at home, but Wynne didn't have the heart to wake him. They could do without him for tonight. She smiled against Callum's bare chest, enjoying the sound of his contented snores. The bed, she decided, was just right.

Epilogue

Forswraithe paced the length of his office. It was a restless, nervous habit, but it soothed his inner beast. That beast longed to break free and run off through the forest, never to return to the stone cage that bound it.

The note had arrived by way of the King's Post, as most did. It was folded in the standard way for letters with an unassuming wax seal. Nothing about it stood out as different or important. The handwriting wasn't familiar, but that didn't mean much. Forswraithe had opened it during breakfast without a second thought and nearly choked on his tea.

He took the note out of his pocket now and read it again. The words hadn't changed, and he crumpled it in his fist. With Ainsley Crichton dead, Forswraithe had thought himself finally free of any obligations—or witnesses—attached to his sins. He thought he could finally be the kind of lord that his holdings desperately needed, not one beholden to outside interests.

You can't change your stars, Gethin, his dead brother's voice taunted. *I told you that when we were young. But you never listened to me, did you, little brother?*

"Get out of my head," Forswraithe growled. "You're not real."

Not real? The voice laughed. *Shall I show you what's real, little brother?*

Forswraithe squeezed his eyes shut, refusing to look at the apparition forming in front of him. He didn't need to see it again. The blue, bloodless lips. The burning, accusing eyes. The gaping hole where his brother's throat should be.

"Go away. Go away!"

He knows, Gethin. The voice became sing song now. *He knows, and he's going to take it all away from you.*

"No!"

"Gethin? Are you alright?" His wife—*my wife*, the apparition corrected—stood in the doorway, staring at him with troubled eyes. She was ready for bed, swathed in a silk dressing gown.

"I'm fine, dear. Just— just a bad business correspondence."

"You're a rotten liar, Gethin."

She didn't give him a chance to respond before snapping the door shut, a quick motion that stopped just short of slamming it.

She hates you, the dead man whispered. *And she'll hate you more if you kill her son.*

"That's why I'm not going to kill him," Forswraithe said, cramming the note back into his pocket. He pulled a crudely carved pendant that mostly resembled a wolf from under his shirt. He ran a thumb over it pensively, his mind conjuring an image of the girl in red. No, he wouldn't need to kill his nephew—*she* would.

Acknowledgements

Thank you to all of the people who helped make this book everything I wanted it to be.

I have to say thank you to Rebecca F. Kenney for inspiring this whole series quite by accident and Michele Quirke for not only naming the first book but encouraging me to continue writing it.

I must also thank my plethora of early readers. Alpha readers: Katherine Macdonald, a queen of indie fairytale retellings; Ashley Evercott; Donna Munt; and the immensely talented Carol Beth Anderson. Your early input was invaluable and kept me motivated.

The beta readers: Midori Anzai, Samantha Eno, Cat Bowser, and Lydia Russell. Thank you all for the timely and insightful feedback. Bared Magic is a stronger book because of you.

Thank you to all of the editors who contributed their expertise; Kate Yelland, Haley Kilgour, and David Balog.

And finally, I want to give a very special thank you to Judah Lamey for all of his incredible work on not only the original cover, but also all the interior trimmings. This wouldn't be nearly as pretty of a book without you.

About the Author

Sara Cleveland is a web developer by day and a fantasy author by night. When not writing or working, Sara is an avid reader and a baseball fan. Her other hobbies include crocheting and playing card games. She lives in Northeast Ohio with her husband and their spoiled cats.

Visit Sara online at www.sara-cleveland.com